THE NEWCOMERS

THE NEWCOMERS

A NOVEL

Lily Poritz Miller

Sumach Press

Toronto

Published in 2013 by Sumach Press, an imprint of
Three O'Clock Press Inc.
425 Adelaide St. W. #200 | Toronto ON | M5V3C1
www.threeoclockpress.com

Every reasonable effort has been made to identify copyright holders.
Three O'Clock Press would be pleased to have any errors or omissions
brought to its attention.

Library and Archives Canada Cataloguing in Publication

Miller, Lily Poritz, author
The newcomers / Lily Poritz Miller.

ISBN 978-1-927513-61-3 (pbk.)

I. Title.

PS8576.I54N49 2013   C813'.54   C2013-903689-X

Design: Sarah Hope Wayne

Printed and bound in Canada by Marquis

In memory of my mother

"A woman of valour
who can find?
Far beyond rubies
is her value."

Proverbs 31:10

Also by Lily Poritz Miller

A Greater Love (drama, Kindle edition)

In a Pale Blue Light (a novel, print and e-book editions)

My Star of Hope (drama, Kindle edition)

The Proud One (drama, Kindle edition)

A Thousand Threads: a story told through Yiddish letters
(print and Kindle editions)

PREFACE

In writing *In a Pale Blue Light*, to which this book is a sequel, I grew close to my characters and there was emptiness in leaving them behind. I wanted to continue to live with them, to follow them through the new phase in their lives.

It was also reassuring to find that many readers of the first book seemed eager to know what became of this family once they left South Africa and sailed to America.

It would be untrue to say that I was not drawing on personal experience in creating my story, but many years had passed since the events and memory can play strange tricks. Also, imagination tends to transcend reality and I believe it reveals the truth in a greater dimension.

Lily Poritz Miller

ONE

Before leaving Cape Town, Libka and Golda sat at the dressmaker's house after school for almost a year as the coloured woman sewed them outfits for the new country—embroidered dresses with capped sleeves and satin bows for their hair, silk peasant skirts with ruffles at the ankles. And Sara had taken them to Adderley Street where they were fitted for red paradise shoes with open toes and black patent-leathers with little heels.

Now Libka was meandering through the snow and mud around the textile mills of southern New England. In Cape Town she would have been swimming at Three Anchor Bay, her favourite haunt, diving off the sleek black rocks into the balmy ocean.

A gust of wind hurled her blazer open. Perhaps she should have worn a coat instead of this blazer from her old boarding school. "In the middle of winter you will go without a coat?" Sara tugged a garment out of the Hadassah sack. "In this country December is winter, my child."

Libka refused but pulled over a cable-stitch sweater beneath her blazer. Her legs were wrapped in black stockings and her shoes were soiled from the slush.

Earlier that winter a heap of garments had arrived from the Hadassah.

"Is this what we came to the golden land for?" Libka protested, her dark eyes blazing.

"*Sha*, my child!" Sara pleaded. "The Jewish organization is here for helping people. They know we are a respectable family. After all, your uncle is a important man in the community."

"Why? Because this whole town thinks he saved his poor relatives! 'Your uncle is a wonderful man!' Mrs. Gadinsky cornered me after school the other day. 'Imagine bringing over a widow and five children—from Africa of all places!' That woman's voice is so loud and everyone in the playground heard."

Libka was a junior at Little Falls High, and Aunt Bessy had urged her mother to plan her future. "She'll never be suitable for an office job with that funny accent. Even at Woolworths, where I know the manager, they couldn't use her."

As Libka heaved open the green wooden door to the mill, she was confronted by the rattle of a cart. "Yes?" A burly figure steered a wagon of dresses.

Libka dug in her purse for the clipping from the *Little Falls Chronicle*, to check the ad for a part-time spinner.

"I'm applying for the job that was advertised."

"Take the main entrance. You're blocking my way."

When she entered the mill, she lingered at the elevator with the metal bars, which seemed like a prison cell. Then she noticed a dingy staircase and tiptoed up, landing in an open area where women were positioned at machines, twirling wheels and pumping their feet. Their faces were painted like clowns, mouths blood red and lashes flashing. Some wore tight sweaters with their breasts oozing out. She still found it shocking to see a black-skinned woman wedged in among white workers.

A brassy-haired receptionist was plugging red cords into slots, chiming "Bernstein Textiles..."

"You looking for someone, dearie?"

Libka held up the newspaper clipping. "I came to apply..."

But the woman was back with the rubbery plugs, chewing on her bubble gum. "Your mother work here?"

As she tried to explain, the receptionist formed a perfect bubble with the gum. "No, sweetheart. We got no jobs here."

When Libka came home, splattered with mud and snow, her mother was sitting on the small wooden porch with only a faint light cast over her knitting needles. A ragged quilt covered her legs. Winter was not unusual for Sara, who had grown up in Eastern Europe. Even so, living in the balminess of South Africa for almost twenty years had conditioned her to milder ways.

Autumn had passed and the blustery American winter had come again. How the children had shivered with a strange delight when they first experienced the sensation of snow.

"You will catch pneumonia going out in the light blazer." Sara dropped her knitting. "Tell me, you had a good interview, my child?" She scampered into the living room after Libka. "I will heat some milk to warm you up."

"Keep your milk!"

Libka dashed upstairs to her room, banging the door shut. She was relieved her sister was not home so she could have the room to herself. In Cape Town she and Golda each had their own rooms, except for the time after her father's death when her mother rented out a section of the house.

But now the family was crammed into this cottage on the dead-end street that her uncle selected before they arrived in America.

"Meyer," Sara said when they entered the small dwelling, "why you buy a house that is only suitable for a couple and maybe one child?"

"Sara," Meyer chuckled, "in America money goes. What you want me to buy for you—a palace?"

This was not the brother she remembered from their youth. Where was the idealistic boy who had left their Lithuanian village in 1923 with the dream of being a writer in America? Where was the brother who wrote such passionate letters during the five years he was stranded in Havana and urged her to join him after Yosef's death?

"How can these children attend an English school with such names?" Aunt Bessy insisted. "In Europe maybe they can be Libka or Golda, but who could pronounce such names in America?"

Libka was now Lorna and Golda had become Gail. Beryl was Bert and Shneyer struggled to remember that his new name was Sandy. Only Dina at three was young enough to keep her own name.

"You have to remember, Sara," Bessy instructed her sister-in-law, "you're living in a modern country and you got to take on the new ways."

Sara's main concern was to provide a good education for her children. Though the family had resources from the sale of their house in Cape Town and the engineering factory, she was aware that funds can swiftly be depleted. She did not feel qualified for an office job in America due to her faltering English. When she consulted her brother about investments, he scoffed. "Sara, I realize that in our shtetl you worked in the bank, but you are now in America, and what do you know about such things?"

"Of course I wouldn't gamble," Sara explained, "but I could invest a small amount in secure stocks and bonds."

"So you will become an American capitalist?"

"Meyer, you yourself have stocks in AT&T, IBM..."

Meyer chuckled. "Sara, a doctor don't prescribe the same medicine for every patient. What can be good for one can be poison for another."

There had been a beauty parlour around the corner from Sara's house that had closed eight months earlier and Bessy suggested Sara set up a bakery there.

"People eat, they always eat, and with all the Jewish families in the area, you'll make a living," she told Sara. "I'll talk to Morrie who owns the store."

She explained that she and her husband had brought over from Africa a widow with five small children, and since Morrie was a member of the temple, he would perform a mitzvah if he leased the premises to her at a modest rent.

"Look, Morrie, you were an immigrant too, and you're not getting rich if the place is standing empty."

"All right, Bessy. Twenty-five dollars I'll charge her a month."

When Bessy told Sara of the arrangement, she asked, "Do you think the American ladies will buy my baking? I can manage for the family, but to run a business?"

"If you make good, they'll buy. I'll set you up. Tomorrow morning we go down to the A&P and we load up with flour, sugar, eggs..."

"How much you think I should bake, Bessy? After all, perishables."

"You can't put two bagels in the window. People like to look around. Maybe they want cherry strudel but they like to see the cheese and apple too, so you got to fill up a showcase. The showcase I'll get from Hymie—he went out of business last month. A cash register also. You can add, huh, Sara? After all, you worked in the bank in Lithuania."

ooooo

The first night, Sara baked five trays of bagels, three dozen rolls, six challah, and a selection of strudel, cinnamon buns, Danish pastry and fruit pies. She started right after the children had supper and puttered around all night as the smells wafted up to the bedrooms. In the morning the dining room table was spread with a white cloth and bedecked with the provisions. They had bought a wheelbarrow from a lumber yard and Beryl would transport the goods to the bakery before going to school.

"I must confess I don't relish passing the neighbours wheeling this old barrow," he commented, "but I guess we have no choice."

Word spread about Sara's bakery. One neighbour told another, and the other told the one across the street, and those who ran into each other downtown eyed the French pastry windows and remarked, "I hear the refugee lady's bakery got good stuff cheap."

Despite the brisk beginning, the business went downhill. Women came and they looked and they touched. "How much is this—that one over there, the one with the yellow filling? What's that, custard?"

"Huh?" Sara sometimes had difficulty understanding.

"The one there in the corner—the one with the yellow filling. Is that custard?"

"Lemon."

"Ah. I want custard. Where's your custard Danish?"

"Custard I don't have. But there's cherry and cheese."

"You got apple?"

"Apple I sell out already."

"No apple, huh? Well, what's that over there—that pie with the crumbs on top. Boysenberry?"

"That's a cherry pie."

"You got boysenberry?"

Sara had never heard that expression. "Like I say, it is a cherry pie."

"Is it fresh?"

"From today."

Leftovers grew. Day-old provisions were offered at half price, but customers felt them and smelled them and declared they were stale; and Beryl would wheel the supplies back to the house for the family's consumption.

Gradually Sara cut down on her quantities. Customers scrutinized the half-empty trays.

"Is that all the cheese Danish you have?"

Sara nodded.

"You don't have any more of that other stuff—you know, with the raisins and nuts? I had in mind getting a few dozen Danish for our bridge club tonight."

Sara surveyed the trays. "Well, from the cheese is still eight Danish, and the cherry two..."

Four months after the opening of the bakery, the barrow was wheeled back to the house for the last time.

"You got to give a new business a chance," Bessy reprimanded Sara. "I ran into women who said you never had this and you never had that. They asked for apple Danish, you showed cinnamon buns, they asked for cheese strudel, you offered cherry. People want what they want. If they pay money, they got a right to want what they want."

They were sitting in the living room on this evening, Dina on Sara's lap. Golda came in with a tray of tea and apple strudel.

"That Gail will turn out all right." Bessy looked approvingly at her niece. "You like your American name? Better than Golda, huh?"

Golda smiled. She was growing prettier as she entered her teens. Bessy winked at her as she poured the tea.

"Gail, I understand you're friendly with the Kupersteins' daughter. Nice girl. Nice family. I know her mother from the Sisterhood. Annette is in your classes?"

"She's in my French class."

"You're in good company, mark my word."

As Golda made her way out with the empty tray, Bessy turned to Sara. "She'll bring you *muzel*. The other one should only be..." She signalled toward the staircase. "She's home?"

"Libka is upstairs," said Sara.

"And still no job, huh?"

TWO

In brooding letters to her old friend Anya Steinberg, Libka expressed frustration over her new life.

> *My aunt, who used to be a servant in my grandmother's house in Lithuania, has become quite a lady. She was an orphan and an American uncle adopted her years ago. I guess my uncle was lonely and desperate when he came to America so he married her. He seems bitter and disillusioned. When he was stranded in Cuba trying to get into America he wrote my mother these amazing letters. He dreamed of being a poet but now he has given up all his ideals. When we first came to America a bag of old clothes arrived from a Jewish agency. I don't think we ever recovered from the humiliation. If my father had been alive, he would have been horrified. My relatives pretend they're supporting us. Their ambition is to impress this community. My mother sent them money for a proper house, but we're crammed into a little cottage while they live in a sprawling house in the wealthy part of town. Golda and I have to share a room. Dina sleeps in a cot in my mother's room. My aunt keeps sending me for job interviews in factories. I hardly know my cousins. They're aloof, considering us poor immigrants. I think my mother is so disappointed at the change in her brother. They were once so close.*
>
> *PS: By the way, my name is now Lorna. My aunt didn't consider Libka a suitable name for America.*

Anya responded swiftly to Libka's letters.

Your life seems even worse than it was in Cape Town, and that aunt of yours is more of a demon than that Mrs. Peker who tried to run your mother's life after your father died. Come to London. You can stay with my sister and me.

Anya had been Libka's closest friend in Cape Town, though they often fought bitterly. She had left South Africa at the same time as Libka and her family, sailing with them on the Winchester Castle to Southampton. She was joining a sister in England.

Libka had never been drawn to America and viewed England as a country where she might build a life. And now Anya was there, and also the Malay boy, Sayyed bin Noor, whom she could not forget. She had exchanged a few letters with him since arriving in America, and she now felt grown up enough to address him by his first name. He reminded her that, unlike South Africa, in England they would be allowed to speak to each other and could even travel in the same compartment in a train.

Libka's siblings were making a better adjustment to America. Beryl had acquired a group of friends who would drive up to the house, music blasting from convertibles, girls with red mouths and kerchiefs coddled in back. And Beryl would rush out, his eyes shining with excitement, and hop into the convertible as it sped away.

Golda too seemed content. She did not resist the clothes from the Hadassah and was pleased that the cardigans and pleated skirts fit her. She even wore the green wool coat and the tan boots that extended to her knees and a crochet cap with a pompom at the top. Soon after entering school, she made friends whom she sometimes invited to the house. They would sit on the wooden steps that led to the porch and watch the boys and the younger children playing on the dead-end street.

Shneyer, who was six, had entered primary school and was proud of the things he learned. Golda would tutor him and was pleased with his progress.

Dina was lively and had to be watched all the time. Sara often kept her tethered to a rope as she went about her housework and hung out laundry in the yard. After school, Golda would tend to her, giving her a snack and putting her down for a nap, freeing Sara to do the grocery shopping downtown.

ooooo

After the closing of the bakery there had been no prospects. As heating bills were shoved through the mail slot, Sara hobbled around the thermostat, adjusting it to the minimum. Huddling in socks and sweaters, the children looked forward to the warm classrooms where their cheeks would flush.

Sara mumbled to herself so vehemently that Libka would be startled. "Who were you talking to?" she'd demand, and Sara would deny that she had been talking at all.

Curdled milk drained from small cotton sacks secured around the sink, and Beryl objected to the sour smell and often threatened to throw them out. "Leave," Sara would demand, "I am making good cottage cheese."

Orange rinds simmered in sugar as Shneyer teetered on his toes to sniff the pot. "Mama, when will the candy be ready?"

"I'm ashamed to bring anyone into this house," Beryl remarked. "It's a regular zoo."

Golda had searched through the Hadassah bag, hoping her sister would not snatch her choices away. But there was no such danger. When Sara asked Libka, "Did you look if there is something you like?" she eyed her blankly.

"Look where?"

And that winter, with the exception of a pinafore and cardigan she picked up in a mill outlet, Libka wore her Cape Town cotton dresses and sandals; and in the blustery days she pulled over her old school blazer.

Beryl was not thrilled with the offerings from the Hadassah bag. "I don't care much for this style," he'd say. "It's somewhat outdated. The pants are not bad, but I can't say I'm wild about that striped sports jacket. Anyway, why should we be wearing second-hand clothes?"

Dina crawled in and out of the sack, peeking and hiding, trailing garments as she pattered along.

It was Shneyer who thought he was the luckiest. He found an ivory jacket with brass buttons. "How do you like these gold buttons?" he asked as he came downstairs.

"Very nice," said Golda. "Mom, doesn't that jacket look beautiful on Shneyer?"

Sara looked at her son with joy in her eyes, fingering the fabric. "A beautiful jacket with such fancy silk lining. I'm telling you, he look like a young prince."

"A prince in old rags," quipped Libka.

"*Sha!* Don't spoil the enjoyment for him."

Shneyer wore the jacket to synagogue that Saturday and as the family was leaving the temple after the reception, a boy ran up to him. "Hey! Where'd you get that?"

Libka realized what was happening and steered Shneyer away, but the boy trailed him.

"Hey, where'd you get that jacket?"

"My m-mother..."

"It's mine!" The boy tugged at the sleeve that curled over Shneyer's fingers.

That evening Shneyer hid in the bedroom, refusing to eat supper.

"Look how Shneyer is suffering because of the charity," Libka yelled at her mother.

"He ate a lot at the temple reception, so he's not hungry. From everything you make a tragedy."

ooooo

That spring a laundromat in the Portuguese section of town was for sale, and Meyer and Bessy thought this would be suitable for Sara.

"It's a woman's kind of business," Meyer told her as they gathered in the living room. "Of course it's long hours—six days a week, eight to six—but the children can give a hand."

Bessy had cut her work with the Hadassah drive short to be present.

"Lorna can come in after school," she suggested. "Gail also. And Bert could take a mechanics course."

"Machines in this business are always breaking down," warned Meyer. "But if somebody from the family can fix, it's not such a terrible thing. Anyway, Bert should be thinking about the future. He's not college material, so a trade for him would be the answer."

"Yosef and I always thought he should have a profession," said Sara.

"What's wrong with carpenters? Mechanics and plumbers?" Bessy whimpered. "They make good money."

"You have to be realistic, Sara," Meyer advised. "I don't see evidence that the boy can make it as a professional."

Beryl had been working at his uncle's mill after school, dreading the menial tasks as his friends fled the classroom for hockey and baseball games.

"It is not so easy when you come to a new country," Sara explained, "and working afternoons he doesn't have much time left for study."

"In America everybody works. Children have to learn the value of a dollar, and Bert has to realize he doesn't have a father."

Though Beryl did well in school, he was more interested in his social life. The minute the bell sounded, he was out of the classroom. He put in his time at Uncle Meyer's mill, then the excitement began. Every night cars pulled up before the cottage. Gobbling down his supper, he would be out the door. If his looks had been promising as a youngster, now they were striking. His dark eyes gleamed playfully and glossy black curls tumbled over his forehead. He was muscular from weight lifting and strode with a confident gait. "Where we heading for tonight, guys? Anything doing in town? Hey, there's a Western at the outdoor in Somerhill. Want to take it in?"

Libka was surprised when a few girls approached her one day

in the schoolyard. The fuzzy redhead asked, "You're the girl from Africa?"

Libka nodded.

"Any relation to Bert Hoffman?" She giggled as she looked at the girl beside her.

"He's my brother."

"Gee! What's your name?"

Libka still found it awkward to use her new name. "Lorna," she said after a moment.

"Have lunch with us sometime, Lorna, will ya?"

"Yes, I'd be delighted to."

"Delighted to," imitated the dark-skinned girl with the red mouth carved in a heart shape. "Isn't that adorable—the way she says delighted to..." She put her hands on her hips, thrusting her pelvis forward. "'I would be most delighted to...'"

Libka smiled, though she cringed inside.

"Tough making friends in a new town, huh?" the girl said. "Well, stick with us and you won't miss out on any fun."

The girls poked each other and laughed.

"I'm Sylvia," said the redhead, "and guess who she is?"

"Yah, guess," said the other. "What's my name, anyway? It just slipped my mind. Oh yeah, now I remember..."

"Ain't she a nut?" said the redhead. "She's Belinda—we call her Betty."

During recess one day Beryl spotted Libka with the two of them; and though he usually avoided her around the school grounds, this time he approached her.

"Hello there, Lorna, how are you making out?" He sized up the redhead and her friend. "Are these your classmates?"

Giggles came from the girls.

At supper that night, he asked, "Who were those girls?"

Libka pretended she didn't know.

"Why not invite them over sometime? Look, Libka, you've got to be more sociable."

THREE

Sweeping the porch one Sunday morning, Libka glimpsed a Cadillac pulling up in front of the house.

"It's Uncle Meyer," she yelled into the kitchen as she shot up the stairs.

Though Libka would scamper upstairs at the appearance of her relatives, she still did not feel safe. From the top of the stairs she would listen to their conversation in the living room. Bessy's chirpy words would travel upward, but Meyer's statements were muted. A time would come when Bessy would venture upstairs on the pretence of using the bathroom, the purpose being to inspect the upper quarters. At the sound of the creaking stairs, Libka would slide into a closet or flatten herself beneath the bed.

Their visits were usually unexpected, as though to catch the family off guard. "We were just passing by," Bessy would say. "I wanted to drop off some gefilte fish."

Sara, who was serving breakfast, untied her apron and headed for the stairs. "Please let them in, Golda. I will make myself proper."

As Golda went to the door, Beryl groaned. "Isn't it enough that I have to see Uncle Meyer at the mill? Why do they keep barging in unexpectedly?"

Libka peered through a slot in the venetian blinds and watched as Meyer and Bessy stepped out of the car. They strolled toward the gravel driveway, scrutinizing the woodwork and the dry grass.

"Like a stable!" cursed Meyer.

"A disgrace for the neighbours," whined Bessy.

Meyer put his hands in his pockets, resembling an undertaker in his starched white shirt. He frowned as Bessy darted around, peering into crevices, fingering the splintered wood. "Neglected, huh?"

Meyer's face twisted. "A palace they can make into a stable."

"And we still had to find for them a home on a Jewish street."

"Ugh!" Meyer flung a hand into the air.

"So what you want from me? They're your relatives. It was my idea to bring them to America?"

Meyer eyed the window of Sara's neighbour. "*Sha*, Bessy! Mrs. Stein is in the kitchen."

They retraced their path as though just emerging from their car and proceeded up the porch steps. Waiting a moment, they pressed the bell.

Within the house there was a flurry of activity. Dina's dress was splattered with oatmeal, so Shneyer was tugging her upstairs. Golda was puffing out the pillows on the living room couch and gathering the candy wrappers and popcorn.

As the second ring sounded, Beryl said, "I don't give a damn, I'll let them in."

With humble dignity, the relatives entered the living room.

Beryl turned on his charm. "May I take your coat, Auntie?"

Bessy looked up at her handsome nephew and blushed. "Oh, thank you, thank you... Oh, hoh, hoh..."

"And you, Uncle?"

"Thank you, Bert. Much obliged."

As Golda appeared in a neat pinafore, her hair in a ponytail, Bessy remarked, "She hardly looks like a Jewish girl. Isn't that so, Meyer? Light skin, light hair... Like a shiksa!"

"She's Jewish, don't worry," Meyer confirmed with a smirk.

Beryl and Golda suggested the guests be seated when Bessy pointed to the ceiling and squirmed.

Meyer followed her gaze. "You see something?"

"Oh hoh hoh hoh...must be a nest there."

"A nest? Where a nest?"

"A nest?" repeated Beryl. "I'll be darned, Aunt. Pardon me, if I may?"

He came forward and looked in the same direction. "It appears to be a spider web of some kind. Well, don't concern yourself, Aunt, I'll point it out to my mother."

"Leave it to your Aunt Bessy to notice such things," Meyer said in satisfaction.

He wore his festive smile, accompanied by a frown as his mouth veered down at the edges.

"Well," said Bessy, "not the biggest tragedy."

"Tragedy?" Sara had appeared at the foot of the stairs. She hurried toward her relatives. "Something is wrong?"

Bessy blushed again. "Bert, you want to show your mother?"

"Nothing serious, Mom. Nothing to be rattled about."

Beryl pointed to the ceiling. "See up there, Mom... No, slightly to the right... There's a nest of some kind. As a matter of fact, it struck Aunt Bessy the minute she walked through the door."

Sara was teetering on her toes, trying to identify the troublesome area. "I really can't..."

"Well, don't worry about it, Mom. Lorna or Gail will straighten it all out."

"But what is it?" Sara was full of alarm.

"Oh, we're making too much fuss, aren't we?" Bessy declared. "Why don't we settle down and talk. There're more important things, right, Meyer?"

She shot a look at her husband and he cleared his throat.

"Part of the problem," broke in Beryl, "is that my mother seems to have difficulty with her eyes. I've urged her to get new glasses."

"Don't worry about me." Sara smiled. "My eyes is good enough. So sit down, everybody. Tea maybe?"

"We didn't come for your cup of tea, Sara." Meyer settled into the armchair. "We have something to talk about."

"If you'll be good enough to excuse me," Beryl nodded cordially. "I was just heading out the door when your car..."

"Wait, Bert!" Meyer commanded. "I think you need to hear what we have to say. Sit!"

Beryl backed into a chair as Sara sunk into the couch and Bessy cuddled beside her.

"You are a well-mannered boy, a pleasant disposition. That is important too. However—and mark my words—remember, I came also as an immigrant to this country. Not a word of English did I know. I had a room in Brooklyn and I went religiously to night school. I got jobs—delivering orders, washing dishes, operating an elevator. Anything I could find."

"See that? Every word the truth," confirmed Bessy. "Nobody helped him. Nobody done a thing."

"That's right," said Meyer, "I didn't have an uncle to help me out. And despite the advantages you have, Bert, you got to be realistic. Your mother is a widow. What is this I hear that you want to attend college out of town?"

Beryl reddened. "It's not definite, Uncle. I just happened to mention it to a friend."

"That's all right for a rich boy with a father, but how can you expect your mother to send you off to college? It costs money, you know, to live in a dormitory, to have meals. Where will it come from?"

"Well, Meyer—" Sara tried to intervene.

"And I don't see evidence that you are a born student. When you go to a college, it is necessary to study, not just run around."

Sara drew herself forward. "Beryl do his homework, and you know he work after school."

"I will talk to you straight, Bert," Meyer continued as though Sara had not spoken. "You are the oldest in your family. How can you expect your mother to support you when there are still four younger children? You are eighteen years old. You should know better."

"Heh heh... My husband's quite a speechmaker..."

"Well, my plans are not definite yet, Uncle. Maybe I'll get a full-time job for a while and save up."

"We will see," said Sara. "Don't worry, Meyer."

"What you mean, don't worry?" Dismay entered Bessy's face. "We're trying to help you."

"As I told my son, I would like for him to get a proper education."

"It's easy to say," snapped Bessy.

"I never dreamed," said Sara, "that the day would come when Beryl—"

"Remember, he's in America, so Bert you should say."

"My husband thought that Beryl should go into engineering. You will remember Yosef graduated from engineering in Leningrad, and we always thought Beryl inherited his ability."

"For engineering you got to study," advised Bessy. "Maybe a car mechanic, work in a garage..."

"I can't completely disagree with Sara," said Meyer. "She is right to want her children to amount to something. But the question is: where does the money come from?"

"All right, Meyer, I will tell you, I might as well." Sara spoke with determination. "Thank G-d so far I don't have to turn to you or anybody else for charity. My husband, he was a successful man in South Africa, and he left us a prosperous factory and a big house."

"Left..." whined Bessy.

"Of course, money goes," continued Sara. "With the sale of the house in Cape Town I didn't make out so good. As you know, people take advantage when a widow have to leave the country. But for the business I got a fair sum, so we don't need charity. I remember how ashamed Libka was when the bag with the used clothes came from Hadassah. And maybe she is right."

Meyer and Bessy looked at each other and then back at Sara.

"We wish you luck," said Meyer. "That's all we can say."

ooooo

As Sara sat opposite Meyer, she sought traces of the boy she had known in their Lithuanian village. Even after they had parted, Sara had always felt close to him. They wrote each other often and Meyer shared his deepest feelings with her. Had the hard life changed him beyond recognition?

Sara knew of his heartbreak when, after entering America in 1929, his influential half-brother Abraham in New York turned his back on Meyer's dreams. Meyer had hoped to study literature at Columbia University, but his brother gave him no support. Abraham himself had arrived on a steerage vessel with his mother and little sisters when he was twelve years old, and when his mother died a year later he became head of the household. Studying nights he had attained a law degree and married an established American woman for whom he felt no love. He had made many sacrifices and believed his half-brother should find his own way.

Arriving in New York penniless, Meyer worked at menial jobs and studied English at night. An occasional dinner at Abraham's luxurious Park Avenue home made him long for the warmth of the shtetl.

Sara was already in Cape Town when her brother wrote her about Bessy Slomonsky from their hometown. She remembered the orphan who had worked in their mother's inn, a pretty child who Meyer sometimes taught to write a few words. *Her Uncle Yankel brought her to America years ago, and she's not the same girl,* Meyer wrote Sara. *Her uncle owns a mill in a town called Little Falls and they treat Bessy like their own child. They would take me into the business and make a man of me.*

Sara was aware of how Meyer had struggled during his years in Cuba awaiting a visa for America and the disappointment and loneliness felt when he finally entered and met his half-brother. He had had such dreams of an intellectual future. How would he adjust to a life with Bessy Slomonsky? Though she had always been frank in her letters to Meyer, she withheld her concern and sent blessings on behalf of Yosef and herself.

ooooo

Temple Emmanuel Honours Little Falls
Long-time Residents

A special reception will be held at Temple Emmanuel on Thursday evening of this week to honour Mr. and Mrs. Meyer Marcus who recently brought to our city Mrs. Sara Hoffman and her five young children. Upon the death of the head of the household, Mr. Marcus assumed responsibility for his sister and family. When they arrived in our city, a comfortable home awaited them, and the local residents took every measure to help them acclimate to the American ways.

Asked why the successful mill owner undertook this, he responded: "Charity starts with our own families. If we want to do good for the world, we must first take care of our own. I know what it is to be an immigrant, and I wanted to do whatever I humanly could to help my family."

Mr. Marcus himself arrived in our town in 1929 after a five-year delay in Cuba awaiting a visa. He married Bessy Slomonsky from Lithuania who had been brought over by an uncle many years earlier and was educated in this town. Their compassion for the immigrant is clearly demonstrated in this recent act.

Four of the Hoffman children are now in school and looking forward to a successful life in America. The eldest, Bert, 18, a senior at Little Falls High, is employed in the afternoon in his uncle's mill and hoping for a promising future. Lorna, 16, may enter a career in the secretarial field upon graduation from high school. Gail, 14, is taking piano lessons and dreaming of a musical career. And the two youngest will no doubt fare as well under the tutelage of their devoted relatives.

Regretfully, the family was not available for interview at this time.

Sara and the children knew the article was forthcoming. There had been several phone calls from the *Little Falls Chronicle* requesting an interview and a photo session. When Libka heard the nature of the call, she advised the editor that her mother was away and she instructed her siblings to say the same.

Sara was ambivalent about being interviewed, but Libka was determined that she not cooperate. "Are you going to announce in the paper how grateful we are that our American benefactors rescued us?"

FOUR

The laundromat that was for sale materialized, although Sara soon had misgivings about it. Each morning she left home before seven o'clock so that she could be open for business at eight. It was on the other side of town, which meant changing buses, and in Little Falls the buses rarely ran. Most families owned at least one car, and the bus service was a losing operation in danger of being discontinued.

"We ought to get a car," Beryl told his mother. "After all, with so many of us... And Libka and I are already of age to drive."

"We are not yet millionaires."

"For three, four hundred bucks you can pick up a decent second-hand model."

"And the upkeep?" asked Sara. "The gas and oil and parts and repairs... When you have a good income, you will buy a car."

The one who felt the hardship most was Sara, but she never complained.

As she went off to the laundromat, Libka would shout, "Your stockings are ripped to bits. And your heels, look at them, all twisted and worn down."

"What should I do—wear a cocktail dress for the laundromat?"

"People laugh at you when you walk down the street. The children make fun of your twisted feet and the way you babble to yourself. They all think you're crazy."

"So let them think."

"You're disgracing us."

Though Sara appeared to ignore these comments, one morning Libka was shocked at the sight before her. It was six-thirty and she had just arisen. Peering through the window, she saw her mother hobbling toward the wire fence that separated their cottage from the woods, a bag of laundry slung over her shoulder. This was the hour that she set off for work, and she did not wake the children. She left the bagels and boiled eggs on the table, and there was always a container of milk in the fridge.

As Libka watched, she saw her mother put the bag down at the railing. Then she lifted herself onto the wire fence as it rocked back and forth. Libka gasped as her mother slung a leg high in the air and carried it to the other side. Reaching over to retrieve her bag, she hoisted it over her shoulder and disappeared in the woods.

For a long time Libka was too horrified to mention this incident for she felt her mother had gone mad. At night she sometimes hovered at the top of the stairs, listening to Sara talking to herself in the kitchen.

"Why do you scuttle through the woods like a raccoon?" she finally exploded.

A bright smile formed on Sara's face. "You see me, huh? You see your tomboy mama?" She bounced around. "It is good exercise. Come. Come with me to climb the fence and you will get skinny too."

"Aren't you ashamed for the neighbours?"

"Everybody still sleeping. And how you know, you mysterious lady?"

"What would you think if you saw Mrs. Stein climbing the fence in the black of night? Wouldn't anyone call a lunatic asylum?"

"I like to walk through the woods...and this way you don't have to be ashamed how your mother is dressed."

After Sara would leave for the laundromat, the children would gradually arise. Beryl had started to shave and he would be locked in the bathroom for what seemed like hours. Libka would hammer on the door. "Get out! We'll all be late for school."

"Easy there," he'd respond. "Nice and easy."

The bagels would scorch in the toaster, the milk would boil over the pot, and Shneyer would mumble that he had no underwear. The fact that Golda was always so quiet and composed only intensified Libka's anxiety. "Don't just sit there," she'd yell at her, "do something, feel something!"

"I'm going to tell Mommy," Golda would reply in a choked voice. "Just wait till Mommy gets home, I'll tell her."

Dina would cry, and Shneyer would spread out heaps of clothes as he searched for underwear.

"What are you doing?" Libka would shout. "Do you have to empty out the whole drawer?"

"I'm looking for my *gutkes*..."

"But those are Beryl's underpants."

"Maybe I'll find it there."

Again she would fire her eyes against the locked bathroom door. "Are you still there or have you dropped dead at last?"

In good time Beryl would emerge, smelling of various lotions.

"Good morning, brother and sisters, next in line...please enter." Seeing Libka's stony face, he'd punch her playfully on the shoulder. "How about breakfast, huh?"

She'd look at him with daggers in her eyes, but she would be there to prepare breakfast for each one of them, feeding them with a motherly fierceness. "Finish your milk," she'd instruct Shneyer and Dina, "and don't leave a drop."

Despite the turmoil, they would all be ready in time. First to escape would be Beryl, often leaving his books behind. Then Golda would set out with Shneyer. In return for babysitting duties in the evening, Libka would take Dina to the Wolfsons, who had three children. As the smaller ones were not yet in school, Dina would play along with them. This had been organized by Bessy, who knew the Wolfsons from Temple Emmanuel.

After school Golda would go to the laundromat to relieve Sara for the rest of the day. Sara would greet her joyfully, eager to head home, her mind full of ideas on how to feed her children. Often she would carry a large bag, slinging it over her shoulder. The bag would contain clean sheets, towels and clothing for the children...and it seemed that no sooner did one bag empty than others had filled.

It was Libka's duty to fetch Shneyer after school and then stop off at the Wolfsons for Dina. She could not join the literary or dramatic club, or play tennis or hockey with the other students. Nor could she adhere to Bessy's advice: "It's important to mingle and fit in. Boys and girls all together."

FIVE

Though Libka had never fit into life in Cape Town, this textile town in New England was just as stifling to her. Most of the girls seemed boisterous and crude—blowing bubbles with their gum, greasing their lips in bright red and flirting with boys. She had hardly been an obedient student in Cape Town, resisting the inspection of hair and nails, resenting the school uniform and ugly oxfords, yet the behaviour of the girls in America offended her.

Libka was aware that her mother suffered even more. While raking the leaves in the backyard one afternoon, she overheard a conversation through the hedge.

"She's still a young woman, but who would know it with the way she looks?" Mrs. Stein was saying.

"Imagine her brother taking on such a burden! You read the article in the *Chronicle?*"

"Her life is no bowl of cherries, but she must count her lucky stars to be in America."

Libka resented their words. She was aware of how much her mother had sacrificed. Sara was just beginning to recover from her loss when Uncle Meyer's letter arrived with the tragic news that the family in Europe had been killed. *With so few of us left,* he wrote, *our hearts yearn to be closer.*

During that last year in Cape Town, a man that her mother knew as a girl seemed to wash away the wailing that drenched the house since her father's death. Mr. Garfinkel had arrived in Cape Town on the same ship as Libka's parents. The men used to play chess while her mother and Mrs. Garfinkel whispered about those they had left behind in Lithuania. The two families spent many summers in adjacent villas in Muizenberg until Mr. Garfinkel's wife died and he disappeared.

Less than a year later Libka's father died and her mother spent the evenings chanting tragic Yiddish songs. Then one day Mr. Garfinkel came again. Libka could not understand the change in her mother. Her black clothes vanished, and she now wore delicate embroidered dresses, and the songs she sang were those of lovers. And on the morning they sailed for America, when Mr. Garfinkel drove them to the docks, she was sure he was crying as he hid his face in a handkerchief.

"Don't you feel sad leaving Mr. Garfinkel?" Libka had asked her mother.

"Of course I feel sad, but in America you will have an uncle and aunt and also cousins."

Libka poured out her heart in letters to Anya.

I think my mother realizes we made a mistake coming to America. She's become so old and neglected. She must miss Mr. Garfinkel. Though I never thought anyone could replace my father, I now wish that he was still in our lives.

Anya wrote long letters describing her new life in London. Her dream was to study literature. Libka was surprised she didn't consider politics, being so opposed to the class system in South Africa. When Libka's beloved Maputo, who had worked in her home, was thrown in jail for a crime he did not commit, Anya was almost as devastated as she had been; and she accompanied Libka on the dismal train ride to visit him at the prison.

If there was anyone who could understand her loneliness, she believed it was Anya.

ooooo

As she had done in Cape Town, Libka turned to the ocean for release from her tensions. She had found a desolate stretch of beach that had been ravaged by a hurricane. The Jewish girls of Little Falls would gather in convertibles and, with hair flying, they would speed off to the popular beach in Newport, where they would spread out their colourful towels and parade on the soft sands. There they would encounter the boys from high school, and they would splash in the water, the boys sometimes submerging the girls who giggled hysterically as they tossed their soaked heads. Occasionally a girl would jump on a boy's shoulders as he raced into the ocean with her.

In the evenings there would be wienie roasts and couples would snuggle together beneath blankets, exploring each other in the darkness.

Only once had Libka gone to the Newport beach. A school acquaintance, taking pity on her, had dragged her along; but her companion was soon mingling with the other girls and boys, and Libka remained sitting on her towel, feeling lost and alone.

On the hurricane-ravaged beach she felt the ocean was hers. It returned to her the days at Three Anchor Bay in Cape Town when she would take Shneyer and they would stroll through the Commons where boys and girls ran three-legged races, then feel the breeze and hear the breakers explode on the shore. There was rarely anyone at that beach either, and Libka would undress into her bathing suit and climb the slippery black rocks from which she would dive into the waters. No matter how burdened her mind would be, the ocean seemed to release her. It was there that she found solace after her father's death when her home was in perpetual mourning. It was there too that she had first encountered Sayyed bin Noor, the dreamy-eyed Malay boy. She had been drawn to him from the moment she spotted him. Was it the sombre look in his grey eyes or the fact that he was always surrounded by books and she had once seen him reading Dostoyevsky, her father's favourite writer? And it seemed odd that she, so shy and awkward, would have approached him.

Their first encounter kept replaying in her mind. She had seen him a number of times, and whenever she turned her eyes in his direction, he would avoid her gaze. Yet that day when she strolled past him, daring him to look up, he had put down his book and asked gently, "Are you lost?" And she had stooped down on the sand beside him, though it was forbidden for a European girl to interact with a Malay. He had opened his satchel and shared the volumes with her. There were books by Churchill, and a book by the spiritual leader of India, Mahatma Gandhi. He spoke of reading it in the original language that his grandfather had taught him, just as she used to dream of one day reading her parents' Russian and Hebrew books.

She had even unloaded her heart—told him how the Voortrekkers had stoned her house in Newlands because she was Jewish. She spoke of her beloved Maputo who was now in jail. And, with tears filling her eyes, she revealed that her father was buried in the Pinelands Jewish Cemetery.

Then, ashamed for pouring out her heart, she wanted to slip away, but he accompanied her through the Commons. "I live in London," he told her, "but I come to visit my grandparents here during my school holidays."

Before parting he handed her a book of Robert Browning's poems. "I want to share these with you." She might never have found him again, but inscribed on the first page was the name Sayyed bin Noor and a London address.

If I can't see him again, then you must, Libka wrote Anya. *Since you're in London, get in touch with him.*

Sayyed, who was a student at Oxford University, took Anya to lunch. *I felt so proud being seen with him,* Anya wrote Libka. *We spoke mostly about you. He thought it was so brave of you to talk to him in South Africa. Are you still treasuring the book of Robert Browning's poems he gave you and pretending you're his secret bride, Elizabeth Barrett Browning?*

Anya had told Sayyed that the letter he wrote Libka at boarding school had been confiscated and that she was put in detention for corresponding with a Malay. *I'm sorry I caused you this suffering,*

Sayyed wrote her. *Why did you keep it from me?*

Get away from that suffocating town and your horrible relatives, Anya urged Libka. *It was hard for me to leave my mother in Cape Town since she was all alone, but your mom would still have Beryl and Golda and the little ones. And you could hang out at Oxford and have lunch with Sayyed!*

Libka remembered how in her loneliness at boarding school she had written to him, opening her heart just as she had done that day on the beach at Three Anchor Bay. She admitted that she did not feel she belonged in South Africa and dreamed of being in England where she heard that people behaved differently. She also wrote about Anya, who was saving up for a passage to England. *If I can't talk to you, at least she will be able to.*

SIX

Don't worry," Sara said, "the laundromat isn't a goldmine but we will make a living. So there is better times ahead."

The occasion for the optimism was Libka's first date.

"Imagine," said Sara, "for a strange lady, this Mrs. Klein, to take such a interest. So you see, my child, it is important to show yourself sometimes."

Under pressure, Libka had gone with her family to Temple Emmanuel one Saturday, and her aunt had introduced her new relatives to some of her friends. Mrs. Klein had shown special interest. "A lovely family. Five beautiful children. I must tell you, Mrs. Hoffman, that I have the deepest admiration for you. You have to be a strong woman to bear such a burden. And your children, each one more gracious than the other."

On the following day Bessy called Sara. "I have some surprising news for you. Huh, really surprising. Remember Mrs. Klein, the lady at the temple yesterday? Well, she was impressed. And what do you think she wants to do? She wants to introduce Lorna to a nephew of hers."

"Who's her nephew?" Libka wanted to know when her mother broke the news exultantly.

"What you mean, who is he? Mrs. Klein—you remember the lady who talk so nice English? She was educated in America I understand from Bessy. And they are a prominent family in the community."

"But the nephew. I'm asking about the nephew."

"Bessy tell me his name is Melvin. Melvin Kaplan."

"So, wonderful! He has a name. But what about him?"

"What you want, a life history? A young man! It can suit you."

"Well, I'm not interested."

"So you are not. Who will you hurt with this behaviour?"

"Have you ever heard of him?" Libka asked Beryl. "Melvin Kaplan."

"Never heard of him."

"You see," Libka told her mother, "Beryl hasn't heard of him."

"He is not a school boy. They say he is a little older. So what?"

"You seem to know a lot more than you're telling."

"I'm holding big secrets from you. Any girl would be honoured to go out with a boy a little older. He can take out in better style, fancier. I'm surprised that he is interested."

"That's a fact," said Beryl. "You make a point there, Ma."

"Of course," said Sara. "There are plenty of girls. No shortage. But apparently this Mrs. Klein was highly impressed and she must have given a good report."

"Apparently," agreed Beryl.

"And the boy, they say is...uh...quite a catch, according to Bessy. He work in his father's business...the only son...a big hardware store...."

"If he's such hot stuff," said Libka, "how come he's interested in a blind date?"

"Who know? Maybe to him it is a novelty to meet from South Africa a girl, and he know the family from good recommendation."

ooooo

The next Saturday Beryl and Golda agreed to run the laundromat, and Shneyer and Dina were taken to the Wolfsons. Sara dressed up in a white lace blouse and a linen skirt and took a bus downtown with Libka.

"After all," she said, "for such occasions I can still draw out a few dollars. We will buy a beautiful outfit for you."

"How much money did you take with you?" Libka asked.

Sara was secretive. "Don't worry."

"But how much?"

Sara nodded confidently. "Any dress in the store you see, if it suit you, if it fit right, I can still afford to buy for you."

They paced up and down Main Street, looking in windows, entering the finer apparel shops that Libka had formerly feared. Clerks would greet them, exuding charm and confidence. Libka wanted to shrink into her skin, but Sara conducted herself with pride. "We are looking for a outfit for my daughter. Evening wear. We were thinking something in a green silk or taffeta."

"Size?"

Well," said Sara, "in the country from where we come the sizes is different."

"Oh," said the clerk, "what country is that?"

"From South Africa."

"Is that a fact!" The woman eyed them in wonder. "Don't tell me you're the family I read about in the *Little Falls Chronicle*—the relatives of Mr. and Mrs. Marcus of Lakeview Avenue?"

"That's right."

"Imagine that! I'm delighted to meet you. Everybody in the town's talking. Imagine! You are Mrs...?"

"Hoffman."

"And this is your daughter? Now isn't that a pleasant surprise." She looked from one to the other. "And may I ask, what is the occasion?"

"Occasion?"

"Your daughter has a special event coming up?"

"No," Libka cut in, "nothing special."

"Whatever," said the woman, eying her with mixed feelings. "You're looking for something more formal. Let's see what we can come up with."

After measuring Libka in the balcony area of the shop, the clerk brought out satins carved to the navel, bedecked with rhinestones and sashes. There were royal blues and shocking pinks, many with crinolines. One had a dazzling brooch at the breast and a bare back.

34

"She'd have to wear a strapless bra with that," the clerk advised of one dress Libka wiggled into. "It's a little snug at the hips. We can take it out on the sides... This one might be more appropriate," the woman said when Libka rejected the one with the open back. "You'd have to take off several inches. She is little, isn't she?"

Libka felt like a huge, wobbly bird as she was steered before the mirror time and again in the hissing silks and satins. Finally, she consented to a green taffeta. She didn't like the groove in front or the festive sash in back, but she felt faint and wanted to get out of the store.

Sara paid the extravagant sum willingly, smiling proudly, and when the clerk asked if Libka required sheer stockings or undies, Libka was surprised to see her mother consider it seriously. "Libka," she whispered, "a pair of silk stockings?"

The clerk caught the exchange, and before an answer could come from Libka she was already displaying evil-looking hosiery with seams and spidery designs.

"This is in fashion now," Sara said. "Such a pair maybe?"

Libka found herself with a pair of spidery black hose; and the moment they were out of the door, Sara trotting proudly with the cardboard box, she said, "Libkala, with such a outfit a pair of shoes you need...satin, to match."

Libka felt as though she were in a strange dream. She cringed at the festive outfit but was overwhelmed by the display of interest from her mother.

By the time they arrived home hours later, Libka had acquired not only a pair of green satin shoes but a little black velvet bag with a rhinestone clutch, a pair of lace elbow gloves and a green silk band for her hair.

"A good investment," Sara announced to the family at supper-time. "She look like a princess in the outfit. The dress fit perfect, just a little long, so I will alter. But, listen, even the most beautiful girls, if they don't take a interest, dress up nice, they also don't look so hot."

"Quiet already," said Beryl. "You've been babbling non-stop about that outfit."

"You should have seen her downtown," said Libka. "She walked around as though she owned City Hall."

"Is that a fact? Yes, I wouldn't be in the least surprised. How much did she spend on you?"

"All right," said Sara, "don't make such announcements."

"Why not?" asked Libka. "Is it a secret?"

"Don't make fun."

Beryl strode into the dining room and pulled out the receipt.

"Did the dress actually cost $49.95?" he asked in amazement.

"Sha!"

"What's the secret?" shouted Libka. "I'd think you'd be announcing it from the rooftop."

"From everything they make fun," said Sara. "Eat already and let me attend to the younger children."

ooooo

At precisely eight o'clock on a Saturday night, a grey Dodge pulled up alongside the Hoffman home. Libka was ready for her ordeal. She had, in fact, been ready for more than an hour, and now the needles of her girdle and bra were stabbing her. She had felt good at first, with all the family hovering around her.

"Can you believe, Beryl, that this is your sister Libka? Look and tell."

Beryl had darted into the doorway of Libka's bedroom where she stood before the large mirror with her mother on one side and Golda on the other, and the two smaller children looking at their sister in awe. "Can you believe that this is your own sister?"

Beryl studied Libka a moment. "No, I wouldn't have thought so... She looks no different from any American girl passing down the street."

"You see?" Sara said to Libka. "Even Beryl say."

"Those shoes too," remarked Beryl, "they go well with the outfit. Harmonize. Hah, no question about it. I wouldn't have believed it, not in a hundred years."

When Libka looked around a moment later Beryl was no longer

in sight, and in an instant she heard a car horn and the back door closed.

"That's a very pretty dress." Golda fingered the green taffeta in reverence. "No wonder it costs so much money."

"Listen, my child," Sara stroked Golda's hair, "for you will also come the day. You will also stand one day before the mirror like a beautiful princess."

Golda sighed in wonder.

"I want my children to have the best opportunities. Imagine, would you believe this is the same girl?"

Shneyer, who was crouching near the closet, stole an occasional peek at his sister. Dina was dazzled by the sparkling green taffeta, and she tried to tug at the silk band on Libka's hair.

"No, no, no," warned Sara. "Don't touch. Come, I will fix."

Sara brushed Libka's chestnut hair that cascaded over her shoulders.

"Maybe you are right that it wasn't necessary to have the hair professionally done," she said, "with such natural curls."

"I wouldn't go near a beauty parlour."

"A hairdresser could make fancier, but the ribbon keep the hair out of the eyes. You got beautiful features, Libka, but who would know with the hair always hiding the face?"

As Libka looked in the mirror, she was surprised at her own appearance. Despite feeling ruffled, she exuded radiance. Her eyes seemed less intense, softened by the flush of her cheeks. She pouted her lips with their pink icing and felt she was in someone else's body.

"The boy will have a nice surprise," Sara said proudly. "I will go downstairs and wait."

At the sound of a car hovering in front of the cottage, Libka peeked through the venetian blinds in her room.

A head emerged from the driver's seat. In the dimness it seemed round and shiny, and she caught a flash of spectacles. The figure that appeared was in formal attire, a man in a suit. It has to be a mistake, thought Libka; and as the form began shuffling across the street, she put her hand to her heart. "Thank goodness!" She fled downstairs, where her mother stood poised to answer the door. "It's not him," she whispered in relief.

Golda sauntered into the living room, followed by Shneyer and Dina who had been spruced up.

Libka scarcely had time to digest her relief when the doorbell sounded. She eyed her mother in horror.

"Don't worry, my child, I will answer." Sara assumed a polite smile as she headed for the door.

"Good evening... My name is Melvin Kaplan." He extended his hand. "You must be Mrs..."

"That's right, Lorna's mother. Mrs. Hoffman."

The man who entered was the one Libka had glimpsed from upstairs.

"How do you do?" he addressed the group. "Now who is who?"

"I will tell," said Sara, her face flushed. "This one is my daughter Lorna. She is the one that you...uh...meeting tonight."

He looked her over appreciatively, then extended a hand. "I'm delighted to meet you. Melvin is my name."

Libka smiled and curtsied. It was the taffeta skirt that created the flourish.

"And here are my other children." Sara tried to remember their American names. "Gail, Sandy and Dina."

"Oh. So let's see... How many are there?"

"My son Bert is not home. I have five children, two sons and three daughters."

"Very nice," said Melvin. "So you must all be thrilled to be in America."

Sara nodded and the children smiled.

Melvin declined the ginger ale that Sara offered; and after some chatter, he cleared his throat. "Well, Lorna, shall we go?"

As she turned, her dress twirled around her and she heard the hissing of the taffeta. "I'll get my stole."

When she came down again, all eyes filled with awe. A white crochet stole bedecked the shimmering green dress, lace gloves extended to her elbows, and she clutched a velvet evening bag.

Melvin took her arm and helped her down the final step and

they made their way toward the door. As Libka darted a look back, she caught tears in her mother's eyes.

ooooo

They went to a club in Somerhill. Melvin ordered a whiskey sour and suggested she try a Pink Lady.

"I'll have to ask the young lady for identification," the waiter said. "The minimum age for ordering alcoholic beverages is eighteen."

Libka fingered her bag. "I don't have any identification."

She decided to get ginger ale, for which she was grateful. She had never tasted liquor except for Manischewitz kosher wine, and she was afraid of the effect it might have on her.

"How old are you really?" Melvin asked.

"Well...eighteen..." she lied.

"I must confess, you're younger than I thought you'd be. I might as well tell you, I'm twenty-seven. You don't mind I'm that much older, do you?"

"No," she said, though he looked forty-seven to her.

Couples danced on the slippery floor, and Melvin invited her to do the fox trot, but she declined, never having danced.

"Let's see, so you're a niece of Mr. and Mrs. Meyer Marcus, is that correct?"

"Yes."

"How exactly?"

"Mr. Marcus is my mother's brother."

"Your mother's brother. I get it. And you hadn't met him before coming to America?"

"No. We always lived in South Africa."

"Admirable. Really admirable. So you children could be considered total strangers to Mr. and Mrs. Marcus?"

"I suppose."

"And yet they were willing to bring you all over." Melvin gestured in awe. "I tell you, Little Falls could use more people like that. No wonder your uncle and aunt are so highly respected in our

Jewish community. But your mother deserves a brother like that. My aunt met her at the temple recently and was very impressed."

Libka sipped her ginger ale and smiled.

"And I understand your aunt is helping you all adjust to the new country. Looking at you, I think she's doing a good job."

Libka wished she could escape.

"Yah, an amazing little woman, that Aunt Bessy of yours. Active in the Hadassah, B'nai Brith, Temple Emmanuel, the Sisterhood. You name it. She's the one who's always coming around with those little blue boxes. Come hell or high water, there she is like clockwork. Nice kids too, aren't they—your cousins?"

My cousins, thought Libka. Who would ever permit that to be known? How carefully her uncle and aunt guarded Ronny and Adele from their immigrant relatives.

"What's your cousin's name again?" asked Melvin. "Ronny, isn't that it?"

Libka nodded.

"Gosh, that young fellow has his whole life mapped out. I ran into him the other day and he gave me this spiel about his political aspirations. Wants to be a senator and I'm sure he'll make it. What's this, Harvard he's got his mind set on?"

This came as a surprise to Libka, considering that her uncle and aunt were so opposed to Beryl and her attending college.

"So you must be thrilled—your mother and all of you. America can be tough, but thank G-d you have such great sponsors."

Libka could not muster enthusiasm for his words.

"Don't get me wrong," he continued, "it must still be hard for your family. I understand your father isn't living?"

"He died...in South Africa."

"He must have been young. What did he die of?"

"The doctors were never sure."

"I guess medicine isn't advanced out there in South Africa."

"My mother sent for specialists from England. They gave my father an injection...a new medicine...penicillin...but it didn't help."

"Well, that's sad, but now that you're in America, things will look up."

SEVEN

It was the height of summer and Uncle Meyer had given Beryl a full-time job at his mill. It had been too late for Beryl to apply to a college for the coming semester, but he was saving his earnings for that possibility. Libka had been unable to find work other than babysitting at the Wolfsons.

"A girl should manage to find some kind of a job," Meyer asserted. "Bessy sent her everywhere—to the Five and Ten where they hire many school girls, for light factory work, which is also not a crime. But nothing materialized. So what will the girl do all summer—just babysit?"

"Well, Meyer, she is not lazy," said Sara. "Anyway, somebody got to be here to take care of the younger children. And with Golda and me mostly in the laundromat, somebody got to attend to the home."

Had it not been for Melvin's endorsement of her, Libka could not have faced her relatives.

"Imagine—my Libkala," Sara rejoiced when Melvin phoned every Monday evening to reserve Saturday night. "If a man like this show interest, it's a good sign. Now Bessy can't criticize so much. His father own a big hardware store, and I understand they have land in Somerhill. And Melvin, the only son, will inherit everything."

"Melvin Kaplan can get any girl," Bessy declared. "Mrs. Krinsky from the Sisterhood told me her daughter, who has a good-paying job in a mill, went out with him twice, but lately he hasn't called her."

As his advantages were stressed, Libka grew to despise him more. She shuddered at the sight of him, at the thought of getting close. The last time he brought her home, he turned off the ignition but had not yet made a move.

Uncle Meyer was also displeased with Bert's performance at the mill. "I am getting fed up with him," he told Sara, his thin mouth drooping. "I don't like to talk this way about anybody, least of all my nephew, but he is forcing me to it. 'Uncle Meyer,' he say to me last Friday, 'I got a social engagement tonight. If you don't mind, I would like to depart slightly earlier.' You know how he talk with the fancy nonsense. 'So why you want to depart early?' I ask him, quite reasonable. 'Some fellows and myself, we're heading for Newport, something's going on at the naval base.'

"'So you got to run to Newport when you have a responsible job?' I ask him. 'It can't wait until six o'clock?'

"I had to put my foot down. No such thing he gets away with from me. And what you think, Bessy didn't see him driving in a convertible with two of the richest boys from Lakeview Avenue? He has to understand his circumstances. What business does he have associating with such people?"

"But to associate with decent people..."

"What you mean, decent? Who say he associate with decent people? I will tell you, Sara, he was seen keeping company with non-Jewish girls." He paused dramatically. "That's right. There are not enough Jewish girls in this town—he got to go out with shiksas?"

ooooo

Beryl's favourite girlfriend was Cassandra, who began pulling up before the house in her yellow convertible. Wearing flimsy dresses, she would run up the porch steps clicking her heels. One Friday evening she arrived when Beryl was not home. At the sound of her footsteps, Libka headed for the stairway. Sara had gone grocery shopping, and Shneyer and Dina had just sat down to eat.

"You can let her in," Libka ordered Golda as she fled upstairs.

Golda opened the door to the willowy girl.

"Bert in?" She tossed her long golden hair and eyed Golda critically.

"He isn't home yet," Golda said apologetically. "Would you like to come in and wait?"

"I might as well. He was supposed to call me at six, and I'm really disgusted."

"I'm very sorry."

Libka had parked herself at the top of the stairs, devouring every word.

"Where is he anyway?" the girl demanded.

"Well, he works at my uncle's mill, but he's usually home by this time."

The girl looked at her watch. "Seven o'clock! He doesn't work until seven o'clock."

"Usually until six."

"I'll hang around for fifteen minutes and that's it!"

She paraded through the living room, snooping at everything, as Golda trailed her respectfully.

"May I offer you some ginger ale or orange soda?"

"I'll have a coke."

Golda blushed. "I'm sorry but we don't have any Coca Cola."

"Then forget it. You don't have to wait on me."

Even so, Golda remained at the girl's side, listening for sounds of Beryl. Shneyer and Dina wandered into the living room with food-stained mouths to see who the visitor was, and the girl looked at them disdainfully. "How many of you are there anyway?"

"That's Sandy and that's Dina," Golda explained, "and then of course there's Beryl."

"Beryl?"

"No, I mean Bert."

The girl eyed her quizzically. "And there's another one—some little dark-haired girl with a ring in her nose." She tossed her hair and laughed. "I'm only kidding about the ring."

"Maybe you're thinking of my sister Lorna." She was relieved that she remembered the name right. "She's my older sister."

"Quite a load of you, aren't there? So where's this place you come from—Africa?"

"South Africa."

"I really mean it, how come you people don't have rings in your noses? I asked Bert and he just laughed."

"We didn't used to wear them."

"Well, in movies of Africa they always have hoops through their noses and black skin."

For some inexplicable reason Dina burst out laughing and this changed the mood.

"Well, you learn something new every day." The girl was digging through the shelf of records by the mantel.

"Those are Bert's records," Golda said nervously. "He doesn't usually let us touch them."

The girl grabbed a handful of records and flopped onto the floor, rummaging through them, sometimes humming a tune. She flung a few aside impetuously, as though to show Golda how unruffled she was by Beryl's orders.

As the back door opened, Golda put her hand to her mouth. "That's him, I think. Maybe you better..."

"Anyone home?" came the cheerful voice of her brother.

Torn between going to him and warning the girl, Golda remained frozen as Beryl breezed into the living room.

"Well, I'll be darned," he said. "How you doing there, Cassandra?"

She continued to flip the records, and Golda was astonished at her courage. She was even more amazed at the pleasant expression on Beryl's face, for she remembered how he had almost torn out Libka's hair when he caught her browsing at his records.

"Any of them you particularly like, Cassandra? Any of them you'd like to play?"

Beryl darted a look at Golda, so she gathered Shneyer and Dina and they rushed upstairs.

At the top of the staircase she encountered Libka's blazing eyes. "Is that the stupid blonde again?" Libka trailed her into the bedroom.

Golda ignored her.

"I recognized that sickening voice from my economics class. Why did you have to be so bloody polite? You should have thrown her out."

Golda opened a textbook and pretended to read. Shneyer and Dina were rolling on the floor in the hallway.

"Leave it to Beryl to dig up the dumbest blonde in Little Falls."

Libka lingered at the top of the staircase, listening to the sounds in the living room. Beryl's voice was more timid than she had ever heard it, and the sounds from the girl were mocking and high pitched. Occasionally she heard a giggle or a shriek.

He has no loyalty, thought Libka. Earlier that week, while cleaning his room, she had come upon a mahogany box from Black Magic chocolates. It was a parting present from someone in Cape Town. Within the box she found perfumed pastel letters from his old girlfriend, Joyce, the beauty queen at the Sea Point pavilion. There were lipstick smears all over the letters and primrose petals tucked in. Joyce had dropped Beryl when she caught Libka polishing the steps outside their house, but when she heard he was going to America, she gave him another chance. Libka had felt sad when the ship veered into the ocean, tearing them apart; but now she wondered whether Beryl had felt it as much as she thought. On the ship he was the first on the dance floor, and no sooner did he step onto land than he was flirting.

Giggles were coming from the living room, and Libka withdrew and went back to the bedroom.

"That brother of ours—he has no loyalty," she muttered to her sister.

Golda did not look up from her book. "You shouldn't criticize his friends. He doesn't criticize yours."

"Who doesn't he criticize?"

"Well...Melvin."

"I think he should criticize him. You've all ganged up on me."

"He's a nice man."

"He's twenty-seven! Why should I go out with an old man when I'm only sixteen? And I still have to lie about my age and pretend

I go to temple services. Do you know I told him I'm eighteen?"

"You didn't have to."

"That's what makes me so mad. I have to lie to please him when I tremble at the thought of him. Every Monday when he calls it ruins my whole week. One of these days I'm going to refuse him."

Golda looked at her as if to say she would not dare.

"Just because Mama is in heaven over Melvin Kaplan, you think I wouldn't spit in his face?"

EIGHT

"A letter for Libka," Beryl announced as he came home from work one night. "Doesn't anyone check the mail on the porch?"

"Oh, I forgot," said Sara. "I came in through the back door."

Beryl studied the blue airmail envelope. "It's from someone in England. An odd name, like the Malay names from Cape Town: Sayyed bin Noor."

A memory flashed before Sara. That was the boy who had written to Libka at Kirstenhof Girls' Academy. She recalled when she had received a stern letter from the headmistress, Mevrou Vandermerve, summoning her for a meeting.

"I guess it's none of our business," said Beryl, "but do you know who this person is?"

"You know also, Beryl. Don't you remember when you took care of the children so I could travel for the meeting?"

"Oh, with that anti-Semite! And you came back as though you had been to hell. That headmistress interrogated you and accused you and Libka of terrible things."

"It was the wrong place to send Libka. Daddy would never have approved. But Mrs. Peker recommended it so highly."

"That's someone we need to forget too."

"Anyway," said Sara, "it looks like Libka is still corresponding with this Malay boy."

"Why would she do that after all the trouble it caused us? They would have expelled Libka if you hadn't withdrawn her from the school."

The back door flew open and Libka popped her head in. She sensed something and eyed Beryl and her mother suspiciously.

Beryl waited a moment then proffered the letter. "For you."

Libka noticed the name and snatched the envelope from her brother. "How come you have it?"

"Can't I pick up the mail from the porch? It's not as though I opened it."

Libka swept past him and ran upstairs. Fortunately Golda was still at her music lesson so she had some privacy. She unglued the blue letter from Sayyed bin Noor.

> *Guess who has retained a copy of the letter I sent you at boarding school? Not that I should be arrogant enough to believe it has any value, but perhaps it proves we will not always be defeated. Anya told me what you and your mother endured over that letter the headmistress confiscated, but it is still in existence on this planet. It is enclosed. So there!*

Libka unfolded the enclosure and read the letter that likely still lay in the archives of Kirstenhof Girls' Academy:

> *Dear Libka,*
>
> *I did not know your name but of course I remember you. What European girl would dare to speak to one of my kind, a Malay, on a beach in South Africa? And, yes, I do remember all you told me that day—about the black servant you seemed to have loved who is now in jail, and how your family was stoned out of your home by the Dutch in Newlands. I had never spoken to a European girl in Cape Town before, so all this was a revelation to me.*
>
> *Now that I am in London, things are different, and here at Oxford I have the good fortune to be considered as a peer among my colleagues. Of course I hold a fondness for Cape Town as my birthplace and I still have my beloved grandparents there; but my parents, both being physicians, could not*

make a life in South Africa, which is why we left for London many years ago.

I was deeply moved to receive your letter and to know that you remember me. I gave you that book by Robert Browning because those poems are special to me and I wanted to share them with you. It was easier than any words I might say.

I'm sorry that you, as a Jewish girl, find life in Cape Town so difficult, but I suppose that the Dutch are also threatened by newcomers, particularly the Jews who have made such a material success of their lives and contributed immensely to the country.

If you should ever decide to relocate to London, please know that I will help you in any way. From this vantage point I will have a right to interact with you and perhaps we can even sit together on a tram or train. That would be an adventure!

Truly faithfully yours,
Sayyed bin Noor

∞∞∞

Just as Libka turned to the past for consolation, so Sara reflected on Abe Garfinkel. She reread a letter he sent soon after she arrived in America.

Not a day passes without thoughts of you. Your parting has left an empty space in my heart. Of course I had no right to influence your decision to join your brother and his family, but life for me here in Cape Town no longer has much value. On Hena's passing I withdrew, but I had to go on for the sake of my children. I was never at ease in this country, and when Andrew decided to study in London I could only encourage him. I felt at a crossroads myself, and then you came into my life again and I found a new purpose.

I should not be burdening you with my thoughts as you your-self struggle to build a new life, but I sense from your letters that your dream of a reunion with your brother has resulted in disappointment. Perhaps it is not too late for us. Shoshana is now married to a fine lad from The Gardens, and Simon has bonded with a girl whom I'm fond of as well. They no longer have a need for me. There is dear Eliza, who has been in our household these many years, but if I should liquidate our home and move to London, Shoshana will take Eliza into her care. The dear woman was like a second mother to her. The business is going well and I don't think I would have difficulty selling it or finding a manager in the interim.

Let me know your thoughts, my beloved Sara

Sara longed to tell him how deeply she missed him and to even admit the mistake she felt she had made in leaving Cape Town; but her response, written in the Hebrew in which they communicated, was restrained.

I remember you warned me that the hard life in America can change a person, and now I understand. Meyer is not the same brother I knew in the shtetl. But my children are trying to make a life in the new country. I have already uprooted them once, so how can I relocate the family again? Before I left, you asked me if it was Cape Town I would miss or something else. I can tell you now that it is something else.

NINE

One Friday afternoon Mrs. Wolfson called Libka. "Can you come earlier tonight? Joel and I have a bridge game at eight, but we're invited for dinner first. Drop by at six?"

When Libka arrived, Mrs. Wolfson was scampering around with pink rollers in her hair, and Libka thought how odd it looked: such a small, boyish woman in grey slacks and sweater with a big head of pink rollers.

"Listen, Lorna honey," she said in her nasal voice, "will you do a real favour for me? The kids haven't eaten yet, so will you put a few things together for them?" The force of her movements drew Libka after her and into the kitchen. "There's some franks in the fridge. Just put them in the pan and heat them up, then open a can of baked beans. Up there, up there...can you reach? In the cupboards up there... Oh, I guess you can't reach. Well, never mind, I'll have to get it myself." She stood on a stepladder and removed a can of Heinz baked beans. "Here. Now if you look in the cutlery drawer...there...there...no, there... Now if you look in there, you'll find an opener. Open the can and throw the contents into a saucepan. Well, what am I telling you! You know all this better than me. After all, you're the oldest in your family, aren't you?"

"Well, my brother..."

"Of the girls, I mean the girls."

"Yes."

"Although I must admit I saw your sister walking down the street the other day and I got a bit confused. She's younger than you?"

Libka nodded.

"I would have taken her for the older one."

She noticed Libka's discomfort. "But that's beside the point, isn't it?" She flashed a smile. "So you'll make up the supper for the children—the baked beans and the franks, and a little applesauce you'll find in the fridge. And don't be bashful. Lorna, you understand that Joel and I don't want you to feel bashful in this house. We want you to feel right at home. So if you have little hunger pangs, don't be bashful. Just open the refrigerator and look around. There's always something to munch on—a piece of muenster cheese, a slice of kosher salami. And you'll find plenty of potato chips and popcorn in this house, with my three little brats...."

The two younger ones threw everything onto the floor and refused to eat. They had red, puffy faces and runny noses. The older boy, Freddy, stuffed potato chips into his mouth while keeping a close eye on Libka. "You shouldn't let them throw the food on the floor," he told her. "If my mother knew that you let them throw it on the floor, she'd be real mad."

"Too bad."

"The girl that was here before—she didn't let them throw it on the floor."

"Then go get that girl."

"She's got a boyfriend now and my mother says she can't bring him."

He looked around sullenly then dug into the franks and beans. "Ooo, these taste horrible. How did you make them so horrible?"

"Then don't gobble so much."

"I'm gobbling because otherwise my mother will be mad. Maybe you don't know, but she can get real mad. That's why she gets the migraine headaches."

Just then one of the children sent a plastic plate flying, and the other followed the example.

"Don't!" Libka shouted. "Don't do that!" She went to get a rag to clean up and turned to see Freddy urging the two younger ones along.

"Are you encouraging them?"

"You're crazy," he said. "But it's no wonder you're crazy because your whole family is crazy."

Libka raised her head from the floor. "What do you mean by that?"

"Boo!" He stuck out a slimy red tongue. "Boo!"

"What do you mean making a statement like that?"

"It's not my statamint..."

"If you ever say anything like that again..."

"What will you do?"

"I'll slap your face."

He dropped his fork and shouted, "I'm not going to eat any more of this junk. And I'm going to tell my mother that you can't even cook it good. Where's the rest of the potato chips?" He flung open a drawer, grabbed a large, greasy bag, and went toward the TV in the living room. "We got a TV set, see, not like you people who got nothing."

Libka tidied up the kitchen, urged the smaller children to drink their milk, which they spat out at her, then she washed them up and took them to their bedroom.

"Now go to sleep."

"Leave the lights on."

"You can't sleep with the lights on."

"Leave the lights on!" came a thunderous voice from the living room. "Otherwise they'll get nightmares and my father will give you hell."

Grudgingly Libka left the lights on. The moment she exited the room she heard movement, as though they were mocking her, but she did not want to give them the satisfaction of noticing. She went into the kitchen and sat down at the table, reading *Siddhartha* by Herman Hesse, which she had recently found in a second-hand bookstore. There were things she could not understand about the world of *Siddhartha* and the strange events that happened to him later in life, but the book cast a spell over her.

"You not supposed to be reading." Freddy stood in the doorway, his mouth splattered with bits of chips.

She just glared, then returned to her book.

"How come you're so funny? Is it because your mother is so funny?"

He could not bear the silence and persisted. "You immigrants? My mother said you immigrants. That's how come your uncle and aunt have to buy you things."

She pretended not to listen.

"Do they buy you all your things—like your clothes and your food and everything? Does your uncle get your books? Did he get that book you reading?"

She nodded without looking at him.

"I wish my uncle would do that for me. My mother says there's not much uncles who would do things like your uncle. How come he give you all the things?"

Libka shrugged.

"But don't you even have a father?"

Libka indicated not.

"Gee!" He stuffed more potato chips into his mouth. "My father, he buys me ice cream. He buys me things. But it's my mother. 'Don't spoil them!' she shouts. 'If you gonna buy them more candy you gonna spoil them!' Your mother doesn't say that to your uncle?"

"No."

"Gee. Then maybe it's nice to be a immigrant... What do you have to do, tell me?" He came close beside her at the kitchen table. "You have to be poor, real poor, huh?"

She agreed.

"Well, how do you get so poor that people have to buy your food? Like do you have to have no money at all—like not even, say, a nickel or a dime?"

She nodded. She was ready to murder him.

"So then you can't be a immigrant!" A bright thought dawned upon him. "My father he pays you. He pays you thirty-five cents a hour, my father does. So how come you can be a immigrant?... I'm going to tell my father!" He bounced across the floor in excitement. "I'm going to tell him that if he pays you so much money, it's not fair that you be a immigrant...."

TEN

"Do you hear that?" Beryl said after supper one night. "Mom said I can actually give a big party. She said we can have it right in our yard, a regular wienie roast."

Libka looked at her mother who was smiling. "How come?"

"How come not?"

"And we're supplying all the food," said Beryl. "Wieners, rolls, donuts. How do you like that?"

Libka was confused. "Do you mind telling me what's going on?"

"What you mean, what's going on?" Sara looked about innocently. "Beryl sponsor with his own wages."

"That's a fact," Beryl said proudly. "Look, you wanna see something." He stuck his hand in the pocket of his white slacks and removed a pile of money. "Watch."

He laid out the bills, counting each one dramatically. "Sixteen, seventeen... Now wait a minute..." He drew out a handful of change. "Seventeen twenty-five...thirty-five, forty-five, wait... here's a 25-cent piece, a quarter, I mean...that makes, uh...let's see... Oh damn, I lost track...."

"That's all right," said Libka, "it makes $17.70."

"$17.70!" Beryl looked at Libka in amusement. "Isn't that something! Uncle Meyer sure doesn't overpay me, but I've put in quite a few extra hours lately."

Libka watched her brother's glowing face, then she turned to her mother. "What's this all about—some conspiracy?"

Late that evening, after Beryl had run off with a convertible of friends, the truth began to surface.

Over tea her mother said with sudden exuberance, "Beryl, thank G-d, is going out with some of the rich Jewish boys. Take Alvin Hirsh, his father a big mill owner, a mansion on Lakeview Avenue. So it is a honour that boys from such homes will take him in. So of course he should do his part. And I will tell you, Libka, you can also benefit. It doesn't hurt for Beryl to introduce a nice, intelligent sister."

"Aha! So that was the reason for the sneaky look you both had."

"What you want from me? I can't give a look without you attacking me!"

ooooo

On a balmy evening the street on which the Hoffman family lived filled with cars and laughter and giddiness. Some cars had to wind onto the main road, and the boys and girls walked up the street, hugging and smooching. In the back yard they saw the fire blazing, and they ran to greet their friends.

Beryl officiated, wearing a white straw hat he had brought over from Cape Town. He was standing by the grill, filling orders for wieners, while people kept popping open cans of soda.

"Help yourselves, everybody," Beryl called from time to time as he passed the franks around. "Lots more drinks by the side of the garage. No bashfulness allowed...huh huh huh...."

The girls surrounded Beryl, coming at him from behind, falling into his arms, pecking him and giggling and teasing.

"Watch out, girls," he'd say, "no questionable behaviour allowed here. This is an official wienie roast, and everyone must be on his best behaviour."

The girls erupted in laughter, jumped onto the nearest boys and flung them to the grass, there to roll and laugh or get a sudden surprise.

"Donuts too," Beryl chimed, "jelly and custard, coconut and chocolate. Get them fast. They're going like hot cakes. I mean hot donuts...huh huh huh..."

The girls rejoiced. The boys grinned. And Beryl was in heaven.

"Come on, Lorna," he called when he spotted her, "how about doing a song for us? Here we go... *Die Stem van Suid-Afrika...*'"

Uit die blou van onse he-mel,
Uit die diep-te van ons see,
Oor ons e-wi-ge ge-berg-tes
Waar die kran-se ant-woord gee.

"Ladies and gentlemen—repeat after me: 'The Call of South Africa...'"

From the blue of our heaven,
From the depths of our sea,
Over our eternal mountain ranges
Where the cliffs give answer.

Though Libka mouthed a few words, it was Beryl who carried the song, his voice growing stronger as the others caught the tune and hummed along. Afterwards everyone clapped and laughed.

As the guests grew drowsy from food and laughter, the air quietened and couples retreated to dark corners, there to huddle on the grass.

In the midst of the turmoil Libka could merge with the crowd, but now in the quiet and intimacy of the night she grew uneasy. As couples continued to bond, her aloneness became more evident. She had spoken to no one during the evening and now she wanted to slip away. But how could she confront her mother in the kitchen when the party was still in full swing?

She could bear being alone, but Beryl had made such an effort to draw her in. "This is Lorna, the African Queen. Watch out, she scratches like a jungle beast."

ooooo

She was an outsider, and she wondered if this was the way she would always be. Could she blame others? Who, for instance, could she blame tonight? She could say they were snobs and patronizing but that would not be right, for there was no haughtiness toward her brother. And they had even been friendly toward her—it was she who always withdrew.

She could not even blame America. How different had it been in Cape Town? Didn't she hide there too—in closets and under tables? A flash of embarrassment passed through her as she remembered a time when Mrs. Peker had found her under the dining room table. And what about at school, hiding behind the caretaker's shed and being discovered by her Afrikaans teacher, who reported the incident to the headmistress?

When did it start? She tried to figure it out. Was she born this way, destined for isolation?

Was it true, as she had overheard her mother tell her uncle, that she became more withdrawn with the death of her father? She remembered eavesdropping from the top of the staircase on a conversation between them.

"She wasn't a lively child. She always used to write in a diary and on the ship to America she wrote poetry. But I think mostly when her father die she became more quiet."

"In psychiatry I don't believe," Uncle Meyer said, "but to me it looks like it's something not right. Listen, I am myself not such a live wire, but when a person can't even look another in the eye..."

"Don't forget, Meyer, she is in America strange and she is a little shy by nature."

"Let me tell you, I'm not trying to make nothing from her," Meyer said. "I don't have to tell you, as a young man I also used to write."

"I remember you wrote articles on Zionism, and also poetry."

"So these things I understand. But there are degrees, Sara, and if a person's behaviour is extreme, that is the point when you ought to question."

"Well, I don't know. She was never a easy child. But her school marks were always from the highest. When she was nine or ten she was already reading books from the adult library. You see for yourself, here in a new country she will graduate from high school before she even turn seventeen. In South Africa she also skip a grade when we still live in the Boer district. The teacher chopped her knuckles with a metal ruler when she discovered she was Jewish, but still they advanced her."

"So your opinion is that the problem started when Yosef died?"

"She was very close to him. Yosef was a wonderful father to all his children, but in the years of his sickness, after the operations, it looked like Libka became the closest to him. The minute she would come home from school, she would run to his room and sit there for hours while he was sleeping, and when he open his eyes she would ask if he want water, and she would rub his feet with the alcohol...."

Meyer was not swayed by Sara's words. "Well, I don't know what to say. She is still a young girl, things can change, but I suspect they won't change much."

ooooo

Libka left the wienie roast before the intimacy of the evening set in. She pretended to be discarding cans and wrappers and finally slipped into the house.

But she held a strange thought; and as she lay in bed that night the thought grew, making her toss and turn until morning. Amid the crowd of chattering girls and boys there had been one boy who seemed to stand apart, who appeared more serious than the others. And it had seemed that his eyes were set on her when she looked his way. He did not come with a girl, though many had gone over and made approaches toward him. And he did not respond to the girls as the other boys had. Throughout the evening he remained apart, and after she left Libka wondered what might have happened.

Visions of this lanky boy with the penetrating eyes lingered in her mind. Could she have only imagined that he was aware of her?

A few evenings later she overheard Beryl telling Sara, "She

didn't do too badly. She made an effort to be friendly."

"She spoke to some people?"

Beryl and Sara would sometimes talk in the kitchen, mostly as he gobbled down his meal in anticipation of the night ahead. And Libka had made it a habit to crouch at the top of the stairs and listen. Her mother and brother were unaware of her eavesdropping, and this was how Libka obtained most of her information.

"There was one guy," said Beryl, "and he happens to be a decent chap, according to what I understand. I don't know him personally but his cousin Alvin brought him along. His name is Matt Hirsh. His father, I understand, owns a big mill in town, and Matt attended private school so he's not much known around here. He's a bit older and goes to college in Boston. Anyhow, I ran into his cousin the other night, and he said this guy would like to call Libka."

"Is that so?" Sara could not restrain her joy. "He would like to call Libka?"

"Don't get so excited. Calm down. You almost spilt the tea all over me."

"I'm sorry," Sara said, composing herself. "I didn't mean to spill." She dropped into the seat opposite Beryl, her eyes flooded with questions. "And he's already a college boy..."

Beryl shuffled his napkin irritably. "I'm sorry I even mentioned it."

"No, no. After all, a mother is interested."

"Now will you pass me a chocolate donut and let me eat in peace?"

ELEVEN

Mr. and Mrs. Wolfson came home early from a bridge game one Saturday night. Mrs. Wolfson was in a foul mood and Mr. Wolfson asked Libka if she would like a ride home. Though she always walked over at the beginning of the evening, when the Wolfsons returned after dark he would give Libka a lift home. "My husband is considerate," Mrs. Wolfson had said.

Mrs. Wolfson gave Libka a dollar and five cents, cheating her of an hour as she often did, and then she said to her husband, "Stop over at the drugstore on your way home and pick up some more Bufferin."

"My wife has one of her migraines again," Mr. Wolfson told Libka as they climbed into the car. Then after he had turned onto the main street he said, "Want to take a ride downtown with me? Pick you up an ice cream at the drugstore."

"Oh, I don't want any ice cream, thank you."

"You want to take the ride anyway, or shall I drop you off?"

There was an ultimatum in his tone, and she didn't want to displease him. "I'll be glad to take the ride."

She tried to make small talk on the trip downtown, and Mr. Wolfson let her struggle in discomfort. Though he was a quiet man, he generally found things to say, and she had never felt uneasy with him before.

He pulled up in front of the drugstore and jumped out hurriedly.

"Chocolate, strawberry or vanilla?"

"No, really," she said, "not for me."

"I'll be back in a minute."

It was nice of him to take her on this ride, she thought. And suddenly she felt sorry for him. Poor Mr. Wolfson with a wife like that...her forehead always wrinkled as though in pain, the concave chest, the nasal voice. And she wondered why a woman would want to have her hair so stiff and prickly, like a porcupine.

And he's not a bad-looking man, she thought as she saw the tall, lean figure coming out of the revolving glass doors.

"Didn't keep you waiting too long, did I?" he asked cheerfully. "You in a great hurry?"

"No, of course not."

The ride home seemed long. He was taking roads she had never seen in her year in Little Falls. There were empty lots, unlit streets and alleys. Occasionally a small amber light warmed the entrance of a house, but everything seemed desolate, so wild and black. She was about to say something when he swerved around a dark corner and cut off the motor, then opened the window.

"Ah! Nice to get some good country air, isn't it?"

He was looking in her direction and she held her eyes steadfastly on the windshield.

"It's nice here," she muttered, and then felt a hand over hers.

"You don't mind," he said, "my holding your hand? My wife and I are very fond of you."

"Oh, thank you."

His silence was sullen, and he kept moving his hand over hers with slow strokes.

"You're a very quiet girl, unusually quiet."

She thought of looking at him, perhaps to ease the situation, but felt that his eyes were focused on her.

"Pretty too. How old are you?"

"Almost seventeen."

"I thought you were older than that."

Even in her discomfort, she couldn't withhold her pleasure. "Really? Why?"

"You don't want me to get...what shall I say...horny? But you've got a well-developed body for that young a girl."

She, a well-developed body?

"And you have a way about you that one doesn't find often, at least not around here in Little Falls. Is that the South African touch?"

"South African?"

"That wiggle. Now don't be embarrassed. It's perfectly delightful."

The absurdity of the situation struck her. Here she was in a parked car in the woods with Mrs. Wolfson's husband.

"Doesn't Mrs. Wolfson need the medicine?" she asked.

"She'll get it in good time."

Abruptly he reached over, and Libka felt his hand come between her legs. She stiffened.

"Relax," he muttered. "Just sit back and relax."

"No!" She tightened as his hand pressed upward. "No, please."

"What are you, a baby?"

Was there something wrong with saying no? Is this what everyone meant when they said she must become American?

"Just sit back and enjoy it. Don't act like a baby."

She started to part her legs, but as his hand bypassed the panty strip, she drew them together again.

"Oh shit!" He withdrew his hand and thumped on the steering wheel. He started the engine and shifted the clutch with such force that it frightened her.

"I'm sorry," she began.

"Everyone's sorry. They're always sorry when it's too late!"

He swerved the car around.

"But I didn't mean to..."

"You didn't mean to what?" For a moment he held the car poised as he looked at her, his eyes flashing with anger.

"I didn't mean to be a problem."

"Well, if you didn't mean to, why were you? You make me feel as though I'm doing something wrong."

"Oh no."

"Then you'll behave?"

She nodded.

He lurched the car forward to its original position and cut off the ignition.

"Lie back!" He released a lever so her body fell back to a supine position. She felt his fingers move her panties aside and enter her, and listened behind closed lids as he panted until she felt something sticky shoot against her hand. He drew away abruptly and as she opened her eyes she saw him fidgeting with his pant's zipper.

In silence he started the car; and just as he turned onto her street, he muttered, "This is something between you and me, right?" And when she looked as though she did not understand, he added, "Breath a word and I'll tell your aunt all about you."

Across from the field where Mr. Wolfson had taken Libka lived the widow Sharon Krinsky and her daughter, Fanny, who worked as a seamstress in a local mill. They occupied the second floor of the tenement house that Mrs. Krinsky owned, and she spent most of her time looking out of the window. On the night when Mr. Wolfson pulled up in the field and turned off his engine, she watched the activity in the car through her binoculars, highlighted by a street lamp.

TWELVE

Now midsummer, Sara sweltered in the heat and dampness of the laundromat and Golda was ever at her side. Beryl went each day to his uncle's mill, and Libka maintained her duties in the home—cleaning, preparing meals and tending to the younger children.

After that article in the *Little Falls Chronicle*, the relationship between Sara and her brother remained strained. Sara never lifted the phone to call Meyer or Bessy, but they would do so on some pretext, making no reference to the event that had estranged them.

One day Bessy's maid was unavailable, and receiving word at the last minute, she had no recourse but to leave her daughter in the hands of Libka.

"I have a busy day at the Hadassah Bargain Centre, but I'll pick Adele up before suppertime. She'll be a good girl."

Adele spent most of the day with a crossword puzzle and other games, and Shneyer hovered around her. Dina was busy with her rag dolls and the garments she kept dragging out of drawers.

Libka was upstairs making the beds when she heard a shriek, "Don't!" She listened but could not hear anything further, so she resumed her work.

Later when she went downstairs to ask the children if they wanted milk and cookies, she found Shneyer huddled in a corner, while Adele was spread out on the living room floor with the Monopoly set around her.

Adele looked up at Libka. "How come your brother's such a cry baby?"

At Adele's comment, Shneyer nestled further into the corner.

"What's the matter?" Libka asked.

"How would I know?" shrieked Adele. "All I did was tell him not to mess up my Monopoly set."

Libka fixed her eyes on the girl, then looked again at the form huddled in the corner. As she came toward him, he put his hands over his face as though to disappear in darkness.

"Shneyer, tell me what's wrong."

"No...n-nothing..."

A cold wave passed through Libka. Her brother was stuttering again. It had first occurred around the time of their father's death...one day when she found him near the rabbit cage behind the house, confused about what the children in the street had said about his father. "What means d-dead?" he had asked.

"He has a speech problem," a teacher reported to Sara soon after he was sent to school in Little Falls. "We recommend speech therapy."

Sara had clasped her hands. "What they trying to make from my children—cripples? Shneyer is quiet, a little bit shy, so he need speech therapy?"

Though Libka was eager to protect Shneyer, she was troubled by this tendency when he was under stress.

"Tell me, Shneyer," she asked again, gently, "what's the matter?"

"Just leave him alone," commanded Adele as she shuffled the game. "What can you do about cry babies?"

How smug she was, spread out in the middle of the floor, while Shneyer trembled in the corner.

"Adele," Libka demanded, "tell me what happened."

The girl jumped up, pigtails flying. "Why you asking me? I was just playing with him...but I told him not to mess up the Monopoly. Because it's mine and I don't want him to mess it up."

A sound escaped from Shneyer, but the word died on his lips.

"What did he say?" Libka asked Adele.

"That's why he's crying—the baby. He thinks it's his Monopoly set."

"Well," said Libka, "isn't it?"

The skinny, long-nosed girl thrust her hands on her hips. "Of course it's not his! What do you mean, it's his? It's mine! It's my mother's and my father's!"

As she spoke she bounced around.

"Now cousin Lorna, don't come tell me you don't know! Everything, just everything in this house belongs to my mother and my father." She ran around the room, pointing at objects. "This carpet belongs to my mother and father, this sofa belongs, this pillow, this table, this chair, this mirror, this lamp, even the lamp shade belongs!"

"Shut up!" The words came from Libka's mouth like a slap. "Shut your filthy mouth!"

But the girl only pranced like a peacock. "You better not talk to me like that, cousin Lorna, because you know what I'll do."

Libka's eyes dared her to proceed.

"I'll tell my mother and I'll tell my father...and they'll come with a big truck and take everything away. They'll take away this chair and the table and the sofa and the curtains and the blinds and the..." She ran from one object to the other.

Libka glared at her, but she knew she held no power over this child. She went quietly to her brother in the corner, and as she put her arm around him, it was as though the tension exploded. He clutched at Libka, the sobs now coming openly. "It's n-not her Mo...nopoly..."

"Of course it's not." Libka hugged her brother.

ooooo

When Sara came home from the laundromat that night Libka wanted to confront her at once and tell her of the episode. But her mother was lugging a huge bag of laundry and her frail body seemed exhausted. "Children," she said, "I want to make for myself a cup of hot tea and then I will prepare supper."

"There was no food in the house," said Libka, "so I couldn't make anything."

"Don't worry, I will find," Sara comforted her. "Maybe tonight a little hot Cream of Wheat with sugar and cinnamon we will add, and for dessert we still got Jell-O."

"Beryl won't go for that."

"He like cereal. And for dessert he will have a chocolate bar. There is still some Hersheys left. You give him a chocolate bar and his mood changes."

Golda looked tired too, pale and withdrawn. Libka feared the dampness of the laundromat was not doing her any good either. She already knew the damage it had done to Sara, though her mother denied it.

"I enjoy to use the heating pad," Sara said when Libka looked beneath her blanket one day. "What you accusing me?"

"What's wrong with your knee?"

Sara got out of bed and hopped around to demonstrate how fit she was. "See? See? And I can still climb over the fence by the woods also."

Libka eyed her mother skeptically.

"I enjoy to have the hot pad after a day in the laundromat."

But Libka knew that her mother was suffering from arthritis.

She waited until everyone had eaten their Cream of Wheat and Shneyer and Dina had been put to bed. Golda was reading in the bedroom and Beryl had gone off hours before. Sara had already taken her nap, accompanied by the hot pad, and Libka heard her light footsteps come downstairs. She would prepare her traditional late cup of tea and browse through the local paper with her dark, saddened eyes.

Libka hardly had the strength to broach the subject, but her mother made it easier when she asked, "So how was it with Adele? She's a nice little girl?" She was pouring tea at the stove. "You want also a cup of tea?"

"A nice little girl!" fumed Libka. "Just like her mother—a sharp-mouthed hypocrite."

"A hypocrite? A child?"

"Tell me," Libka said as Sara put their tea before them and sat down, "did you notice anything strange about Shneyer tonight?"

"I was wondering why he hardly touched his cereal. Maybe he is running a temperature. His forehead was a little hot."

"You know why?"

"What you looking with the wild eyes?"·

"Well, the nice little girl is responsible."

"Tell me plain," said Sara. "Stop making the dramas."

"They're rotten. The whole family is rotten. They only want to capitalize on us—the poor relatives that they brought from Africa. You should have heard how the nice little girl talked today."

When Libka finished the story, a new energy seemed to have entered Sara's body. "I will tell my brother plain, straight to his face."

ooooo

Sara phoned Meyer the following day and now he, Bessy and Adele were assembled in Sara's living room. On this hot Sunday afternoon Libka and Golda had taken the younger children to a local beach, and Beryl was off in Cassandra's car.

"Imagine!" said Bessy. "Cousins! First cousins. You leave them together for a few hours and already there's trouble."

"Like I tell you," said Sara, "the trouble is not with the children. It look to me like the trouble is with the grown-ups."

Bessy shrugged in mock laughter and looked at her husband. "So we are the guilty parties, Meyer?"

"So it seems," he said smugly, a twisted grin on his face. "So it looks like."

"Why you want to shame us so much and make us look so poor? My children, after all, got to make a life for themselves, and they are also proud. Why not? My husband, he was a successful and dignified man. My children are not used to being charity cases."

Bessy snickered. "See that! You try to do a good deed and what happens, you're misunderstood. Huh! I'll tell you the truth, I'm sorry I ever got involved in this."

"*Sha*, Bessy," said Meyer, "let me talk. Sara, put for a moment aside the stories you get who knows from where. Adele say the Monopoly set is hers?"

"That's all," squeaked the girl. "I swear to God, that's all I said. And then he starts to cry."

"Quiet, Adele. You don't talk."

"But he's such a cry baby!"

"Sara," said Meyer, "do you think that Bessy and I would like to do you and your children harm?"

He eyed Sara with astonishment and waited for an answer.

"Well," Sara said, moving uncomfortably on the sofa, "of course I wouldn't think so, but it seems there is proof."

"Proof!" The word burst from the mouths of both parties.

"Huh," said Bessy, "what do you mean proof?"

"I tell you already," said Sara.

"You know what I think," said Meyer with sudden vigour. "I think that a certain member of your family has been poisoning your mind."

"See that, see that," came from Bessy. "That's what Meyer and I think."

"It's cousin Libka," squealed Adele. "She's a troublemaker."

"Shh, shh, shh," said Bessy. "Didn't you hear what your father said—not to interfere?"

"That's right," said Meyer. "We think that she has been instrumental in giving you this impression."

"What you mean instrumental?" Sara was adamant. "She told me plain. She hear with her own ears."

Bessy's mocking laughter came again. "She hears!"

"You have to consider," said Meyer, "from who you get the information. Every person interpret in his own way."

"All right. Maybe Libka is...uh...dramatic...a little too proud, but she don't tell lies. Once before she tell me what the Wolfson boy say. And, after all, people read the paper and they know the honours you get for your generosity. You already have the certificate from the synagogue."

"What do you want me to say?" Meyer exclaimed. "You want me and Bessy to bow our heads and say we are guilty, that I brought over my sister and her five children for my own success and glory?" Proud of his words, he grinned crookedly at Sara.

"Hah hah hah," chuckled Bessy, "that's what it looks like they're thinking."

"What you want me to do," he continued, "to print in the temple bulletin a notice that I disclaim any responsibility for my sister and her family?"

ooooo

It was not wise to reveal that there was tension between the families, so Meyer and Bessy tried to gloss over their disputes and create an impression of harmony. At Sisterhood meetings, Bessy would put in a word to Melvin Kaplan's aunt. "You performed a mitzvah," she would say, loud enough for the other women to hear. "Your nephew Melvin and my niece have hit it off. They're keeping company, the young ones."

Among this group was Sharon Krinsky, who had spied Libka in the parked car in the field with Mr. Wolfson. Much as she ached to reveal this, she restrained herself. The Wolfsons were active in the synagogue and respected in the community. Yet she felt that Mrs. Klein, who was responsible for the introduction, should know the company her nephew was keeping.

Until Melvin met this girl, he had seemed interested in her daughter. Though Fanny was already thirty-two, she was American born and had a steady job at the mill.

How could she reveal what she had witnessed that night without disgracing the Wolfson family? She discussed it with Fanny, who advised, "Maybe we should tell Melvin in secret. Do you want me to do it?"

Mrs. Krinsky did not consider this good strategy. "It would look like you're trying to get him back, Fanny."

THIRTEEN

About a month after the wienie roast, Matt Hirsh reached Libka on the phone. Though she tried to hide her excitement, she had been walking on air since that call.

"We didn't get a chance to talk that night," he said. "I got your number from my cousin Alvin."

Perhaps there was some strange power of communication, she reflected, for he had often been in her thoughts.

She would not dress up for her date with Matt, as she did with Melvin Kaplan. There was something profane about the hissing fabrics and the spidery hose. And a painted face. The more lavish the attire, the more she felt removed from her true self. And though she had only exchanged a few words with Matt during the phone call, she wanted to be real with him—not the frilly and feathery creature she was with Melvin.

Matt wore khakis and a white sweater. He looked even more aesthetic than she remembered. He leaped up the front steps, leaving the engine on in his convertible. "Ready?"

She dashed down the steps, forgetting to say goodbye to the family, and within seconds they were coasting through the mild evening, the music wafting in the air, drowning out any need for talk.

They seemed to drive for hours through the balmy night, and occasionally she glanced at Matt. He had a dreamy look that reminded her of Sayyed bin Noor.

"Anywhere special you'd like to go?" The words came over the music and the wind.

Their eyes met for a moment as she indicated not.

The car gained momentum and now they were racing across bleak highways, passing farms and motels. Sometimes he veered into dirt lanes and she was filled with joy and fear, but then he would swerve onto the highway again.

He took her to an outdoor theatre where a few Westerns were playing. The area was vast and he pulled up near the back, apart from other cars.

"Want some popcorn or candy?" When she declined, he hopped out and came back with his own supplies. He released the front seat, then settled back to watch the movie.

At intermission he asked again if she wanted anything. This time he vanished for so long that she feared he would not return.

He came back just as the second movie was beginning and hastily asked if everything was all right.

"Just fine. It was a very good movie."

As though seeing through her façade, he focused on the screen and adjusted the sound on the speaker.

Minutes before the second film ended, he had his motor running and was the first to cut out of the maze and enter the highway.

Driving through the darkness she felt strained and helpless. She had longed for him to acknowledge her. On the night of the wienie roast he had fixed his eyes upon her, as though recognizing something, but now he hardly looked at her.

Perhaps he was expecting something from her. Perhaps she should reach out and talk to him. Though the radio was no longer on, the speed of the convertible and the intensity with which he focused on the road made any conversation impossible. Only when he pulled up before her house did he glance at her. "It was nice of you to come," he mumbled, then waited until she made her way onto the porch before driving off.

ooooo

The night with Matt Hirsh tormented Libka. Each time the phone rang in the ensuing days she answered with a vague hope that it was him. She watched her brother with Cassandra. They seemed so joyful together, so natural. There appeared to be no mysteries that clouded their minds. Cassandra would often call. "Bert home?... Have him call me when he gets in."

Cassandra arrived frequently in her yellow convertible. She'd hoot three times, and that was the signal for Beryl. Once when she appeared on the porch unannounced and Beryl ran out excitedly, she heard Cassandra yell, "For goodness sake, you keep saying you'll call, and then I have to end up calling you. Watch out or I'll drop you like a ton of bricks!" Then she heard smooching and she knew her brother approved of Cassandra talking that way. He was proud of her and the way her long golden hair harmonized with the car.

"What do you think of her?" he asked Golda. "Would you say she's beautiful?"

When Golda agreed, Beryl promised they would take her for a ride in the convertible.

Libka could never dream of calling a boy. Imagine if she would say, "Why haven't you called me?" Why, she wondered, did she feel she had to maintain this passive role? It may be that Matt was shy, and it must have taken courage for him to call her.

ooooo

Libka was relieved when summer drew to a close. It was a time of convertibles and wienie roasts and golden bodies huddled on soft, white sand. How she had craved for the ocean that summer. She thought of Muizenberg, of the villa they used to rent when her father was alive, sinking her toes through the silky sand and plunging into the breakers. The ocean had always given her a power, a magic; and when on the summer days in Little Falls the convertibles would speed by as she plodded to the laundromat or cared for her siblings, a sense of sadness passed through her.

Sometimes she had gone to the local beach with her little brother and sister—a beach with muddy brown sand and the smell of beer. Rough boys hung around girls who lay in two-piece bathing suits and necked with them. She would feel embarrassed and find a spot away from the litter of cans and cigarette butts. She despised this beach, yet the children splashed in the filthy water with delight. Shneyer had also discovered a concession there.

"Can I have ice cream?" he would ask Libka. "The man said it's ten pennies. How much is ten pennies—a tickey?"

"You're getting mixed up again, Shneyer. We're not in South Africa anymore."

"Oh, I forgot. Not a tickey—a dime?"

"Here's two dimes. Get Dina an ice cream too."

The ice cream would drip down the children's chins, and Libka would feel old and abandoned. She would plunge into the tepid waters and watch the children play near the shore, seaweed wrapped around their feet. When the sun weakened, she would help them dress, pull over her shorts and top, and they'd make their way up the steep incline to the main street. Damp and sticky, they would sometimes wait over half an hour for a bus, then transfer to another, and come home starved and exhausted.

FOURTEEN

September came and it was time to return to school. Libka would be entering her senior year at Little Falls High and Beryl would continue to work full time at his uncle's mill.

"How come you're still here?" Beryl asked Sara as he went into the kitchen. "Aren't you opening the laundromat today?"

"That's all right. I made another arrangement. The first day of the new school year I can still be here to let out my children. And don't worry, Beryl, you won't have to work in Meyer's mill your whole life. We will make a plan for you to go to college." She looked up at her son in pride. He wore the white pants he seemed unable to part with and the white cable-stitch sweater she had knit him. His black shoes were polished to a sparkle and curls hung over his forehead.

"How about breakfast, Mom?"

As Beryl sat down, Golda appeared at the foot of the stairs.

"Well, look how nice she looks," said Beryl. "Not bad. Not bad."

Golda was dressed in a checkered skirt with pleats, and she wore a yellow cardigan and olive knee socks to match her brown shoes.

"Such a pretty girl," said Sara. "Come, darling, sit down to breakfast."

Next came Shneyer, stomping down the stairs in his new brown shoes. "Look! They fit." He put out a foot so Sara could tie the laces. "It fits good, Mama." His golden hair hung to his shoulders in ringlets.

"You really should cut his hair," said Beryl. "The kids make fun of him."

"Such beautiful locks," said Sara. "It seems a shame to chop it off."

"I don't care if they laugh." Gentleness shone in Shneyer's azure eyes. "But you can cut it off if you like."

Sara tied his laces and looked up at him. He stood proudly in his new blue corduroy pants and the blue-and-white striped sweater she had knit. "How do you like my belt?" he asked.

There was a thump and Dina landed beside him.

"Oy yoy yoy, look!" shouted Sara, clapping her hands.

"Golly!" Beryl chuckled. "This is a regular parade."

Golda had dressed the child in a pink knitted outfit and black patent leather shoes with pink socks. Golda ran to her and lifted her skirt. "I knew it! I told her not to take her pants off and she did it again."

"She don't like to wear panties, it seems," said Sara.

Beryl chuckled again. "Golly. Now, Ma, will you pass me some toast and oatmeal? And don't scrape it from the bottom of the pan."

"Fresh oatmeal I make. Not one drop is burnt."

"For a change." Beryl cleared an area for the cereal.

"Do you have a spoon…sugar…milk…a knife…? In this house a person has to ask for everything separately."

"All right, all right," said Sara. "No emergency."

When everyone was seated, gobbling down their oatmeal, a form appeared soundlessly on the landing.

"Libka!"

She wore a red wool dress with lipstick to match. Silver buckles gleamed on her black shoes and she straightened the seam of her sheer stockings.

"Look who is here," said Sara. "Can you believe?"

"Pretty good!" Beryl took in the sight. "Pretty good. Huh! How d'you like that?"

"What's this—a field day?" Libka asked her mother. "Keeping the laundromat closed in honour of school?"

"It is worth any price to see my children so beautiful and well mannered."

"Quiet!" Libka demanded as she saw tears spring to her mother's eyes and felt the same in hers.

"I mean it," Sara continued in a cracked voice as she bustled at the stove. "Daddy should only have lived to see this."

"Do you have to get dramatic again!" Beryl grumbled. "Come on! Will somebody give me a glass of milk and a Hershey bar? I'd like to get out of here already."

"Coming up! Coming up!" Sara laughed through her tears. "One, two, three, coming up!" She darted to the fridge. "Libkala, you get for him the Hershey bar from the cupboard. You are in charge of refreshments."

With the chocolate melting in his mouth, Beryl felt appeased.

"You're right, Mom. We don't have to take any garbage from anyone. You can tell just by looking at us that we have class." As he rose from the table, he rumpled Libka's hair. "Even this one, surprisingly enough."

"You see?" Sara made eyes at Libka. "Even your brother admire."

○○○○○

That day Libka tried to make a good start, though she felt foolish going to school with red lips and sheer stockings. She walked awkwardly in her new shoes with the tiny heels, her legs feeling bare in the hose. Other girls seemed natural and moved with grace.

The first class was economics, a subject she despised. It couldn't possibly be as dull as the teachers made it, she thought. She remembered the monotone voice of last year's teacher, how her mind would wander miles away and suddenly she would be startled at the sound of her name. Usually it had been called several times before she became aware of it, and heads would be turned to her. Then she would not know the question, and sometimes the class would burst out laughing at her dazed state. Yet the teacher had passed her, for she had managed to memorize the facts a day before the exam. How strange the mind is, she thought. She had remembered all the facts for that day, and the very next day she had wiped them from her mind. She somehow did not want to clutter up her head with things that she felt were meaningless. It was different with the books she selected from second-hand stores and read in bed at night. They brought to the surface things that deep within her she had always known.

When she went into her economics class she noticed a girl from last year. She smiled and took a seat beside her. The girl continued scribbling in her notebook.

Only two vacant seats remained in the class, one of them beside Libka. She wanted to lose herself in the crowd, but the teacher was pointing and counting the students.

She struggled through the break between classes and grew tense when the bell rang for lunch. On this first day of school everyone was brimming with excitement, recognizing faces they had not seen all summer, comparing notes on their new teachers and courses.

She stood in the playground, watching the colourful figures gravitate to each other, laughing, chattering and hugging. The air was alive with joy and reawakening. Occasionally she would see a familiar face and try to make conversation, but with her approach the person would vanish. She had not had lunch, for she did not want to go into the cafeteria where she would feel conspicuous. Perhaps she would take her mother's advice and bring a sandwich, but where could she eat it and not be caught munching on pumpernickel bread with salami wedged in? The memory of hiding in lavatories in her Sea Point school days rushed back and she recalled when Anya had discovered her as she sneaked out of a cubicle on the day her first period began. When Anya detected the stain on the back of her white gym shorts and taunted her, a fight had ensued, resulting in Libka's expulsion from school.

"Did you have lunch?"

Libka turned to see Golda with a girl beside her. "Did you?" she blurted.

"We ate in the cafeteria. I had a cheese sandwich and chocolate milk."

Golda's friend smiled, revealing braces over her teeth.

"This is Judy," Golda said politely. "She's in my French class. And this is my sister Lorna."

Libka poked Golda and whispered, "Don't cling to me like that."

"Who's clinging?"

"Go away!"

As Golda and her friend withdrew, Libka wandered around the playground, trying to merge with the animated cliques, and found herself beside a fuzzy redhead.

"So he makes a pass and I let him make a pass," the girl rambled on to a dark-skinned girl who looked Portuguese, "and then he makes another pass, and just when he thinks he's gonna get me, I let him have it." She threw her head back and laughed.

Libka recognized the girls from her history class.

"Sorry about that!" The redhead eyed Libka. "Hey, you're the girl from Africa, right?"

Libka nodded.

"Yeah, you people are famous. I read about you in the *Little Falls Chronicle*. How is it in Africa? Everyone thought you'd have rings in your noses."

"Don't tease her," said the other girl. "We all come from somewhere. Like my people, we're from the Azores. The boat used to land here in Little Falls."

"I'm an imported product too," said the redhead. "I'm French. Can't you tell?" She wiggled. "My people came from the Magdalen Islands in Quebec."

"It's them factories," said the Portuguese girl. "They come here to work in the textile mills."

"So, anyway," the redhead cut in, "like I was saying, pussycat them and promise them everything but give them...hah hah hah..."

"Nothing is what she means," the other explained to Libka. "The guys can crawl all over you, but don't give them an inch. End up in a parked car and the whole of Little Falls knows by the next morning."

Did they know something about her? Had word spread of that

night when Mr. Wolfson took her into the field and warned her never to breathe a word of it?

ooooo

After that episode she had considered no longer babysitting for the Wolfsons, but she thought of the problems it would create. There'd be no place to leave Dina when Sara went to the laundromat and they all set off for school. And Aunt Bessy was ready to pounce on her for everything. So she continued but dreaded the harsh looks from Mr. Wolfson. Even his wife seemed angry and was getting more demanding.

"I have a stack of laundry to the ceiling," she said soon after that night. "Lorna, since you're sitting here anyway, the time will pass faster if you put a few strokes to the wash. The ironing board is all set up for you. I even put water in the iron, and there's a cloth for the silks so you don't iron right on top of them. And my husband, he likes his shirts done with steam and starched."

"She's asking me to do all her housework," Libka complained to her mother. "At first it was only helping with supper, but now she leaves a sink full of dirty dishes and all evening I have to iron."

"You should not do that," Sara said. "Babysitting is one thing, but to clean another person's house..."

"The minute I walk in the door she's giving me orders. And the children are so wild and they know they can get away with it."

"Tell her plainly, my Libkala, that your mother don't permit you to do housework. Tell her you are a girl from an established family in South Africa, and you are used to having servants, and your mother don't allow it."

Yet Libka was afraid to stir up trouble. Mrs. Wolfson seemed more enraged than usual and her husband sometimes looked at Libka with steely eyes, though most of the time he avoided her. Did they share some secret about her?

Though she tried to dismiss that terrible night from her mind, she was filled with fear and revulsion. It recalled an event in her father's factory when she was fourteen. Mr. Shmerl, a friend of her parents from Lithuania who had taken over as manager after her father's death, had lured her up the murky stairs to the rooms where she lived as a small child. He had tried to get her to lie on the mattress, telling her not to behave like a baby. She was afraid to upset him but he drew her close and stuck his tongue into her mouth.

She had never told anyone about the event. Her mother sensed that something had happened, but Libka was unable to reveal it. She felt she may be blamed for what happened, as she was for everything that went wrong in the household after her father's death. And maybe she was responsible. Why had she dressed up like that when she went to the factory? Once before, when Mr. Shmerl had found her alone in the house, he had brushed his leg against her as they sat on the settee and she had caught an evil glint in his eye. She should have known better than to dress up like the women in the cinema.

She had not even been able to share the episode with Anya. Even a year later, when Anya visited her at boarding school and called Mr. Shmerl a sex fiend, she could not unload her heart.

In writing Anya about Mr. Wolfson, she confessed to the secret she had kept within her. *I was never able to tell you what Mr. Shmerl did to me, but it's easier from afar. When I was fourteen he took me up to the rooms above the factory where I lived as a child. He tried to get me down on the dirty mattress and stuck his tongue into my mouth.*

I'm disappointed in you, Anya replied. *What are friends for if not to share such things? Well, at least now you're confiding about Mr. Wolfson. Tell your mother what's going on and get out of that den of iniquity.*

Libka was afraid to be too rash, but the next time Mrs. Wolfson thrust a vacuum cleaner in her hands and cautioned her not to miss under the beds, she muttered, "My mother said I'm not allowed to clean."

The bony woman with the stiff nest of hair acted as though she hadn't heard. "It has two settings—this one you use for the thick carpeting. And there's a brush for the drapes." Then she looked at

Libka. "Did you say something?"

"My mother said I shouldn't clean."

"I have a maid," Mrs. Wolfson retorted. "I'm suggesting you just help tidy up, light things. Do you think I would ask a Jewish girl to do my housework?" Her face was sour. "I promised your Aunt Bessy I would give you this job, and I hope your family appreciates it. There are American girls who would die for the opportunity."

Libka felt foolish afterwards. Had she made a big thing over nothing? It was true, a woman used to come in to help Mrs. Wolfson. She had seen her a few times when she went to get Dina after school. But she hadn't been there since Libka started ironing and doing the dishes and vacuuming the rooms.

"Now I'm not going to ask you to do a thing," Mrs. Wolfson said a few days later. "There's a stack of laundry, but don't touch a thing if your mother doesn't allow it."

By the end of the evening Libka had ironed all the garments.

She grew to despise the Wolfsons. She might have spoken up, but there were too many factors involved. Of the many interviews her aunt had arranged, Mrs. Wolfson was the only one who had taken a chance on her. Also, Dina was used to being left with them. At first she had shrieked when Libka dropped her off, but now she didn't even look behind when Libka slipped away.

But, most of all, what would her aunt say if this job didn't work out? She and Mrs. Wolfson saw each other at temple services and were members of the Sisterhood. Who knows what rumours Mrs. Wolfson might spread?

ooooo

Despite Libka's trepidation, her job at the Wolfsons ended. Perhaps she had been especially sensitive, but when Mrs. Wolfson had rattled the vacuum cleaner toward her, showing her the various notches and brushes, Libka had withdrawn. "I'm sorry, Mrs. Wolfson, but like I said, my mother really doesn't allow me to do heavy housework."

For a while previous to this, Mrs. Wolfson's approach had

changed. She would carry on about why Libka shouldn't bother to iron the laundry stacked on the board or why she shouldn't wash the greasy dishes in the sink. But she could not restrain her compulsion to give orders.

From the way in which Mrs. Wolfson looked at her this time, Libka sensed that the end was near. A few times during the evening, after she had fed the children and put them to sleep, she hovered around the vacuum cleaner, wondering whether she should do the rooms, but she was afraid to wake the children. And the way Freddy tormented her, daring her not to clean his house and maliciously scattering popcorn, further restrained her.

When the Wolfsons returned that evening, they seemed unusually cheerful and friendly.

"How was it, dear?" Mrs. Wolfson asked. "I hope the children didn't give you any trouble."

"No, they were fine."

"I'm so glad because we'd feel terrible if we thought they gave you any trouble."

Was there sarcasm in her tone?

"Now my husband will pay you and he'll give you a lift to your door."

She had never before verbalized this, and it made Libka wonder again.

Mr. Wolfson did not say anything until he approached Libka's house. "Uh, I should tell you that a relative of my wife's is coming to stay with us for a while, so we won't need your services for now."

Libka had avoided any display of emotion and covered up by thanking Mr. Wolfson excessively for the ride. She would have liked to withhold the blow from her mother but was worried where they would leave Dina the next day.

"You don't need their few dollars, my child," Sara said when Libka entered her bedroom and broke the news. "We will make other arrangements. You don't have to be a servant to them. Melvin Kaplan is a more important man than this Mr. Wolfson, and you don't have to lower yourself for anybody."

FIFTEEN

"So I hear your daughter is in the market for a job," Bessy announced on the phone a few days after Libka's babysitting role ended. She had rarely called since the confrontation over Adele, and Sara suspected any word from her would be bad news. She sometimes yearned to unload her heart to her relatives but knew it would not bring any comfort.

"To say I was astonished is not even the word," said Bessy. "It seems that your daughter has become quite a prima donna. From what I hear from Mrs. Wolfson—and I know that woman long enough not to question her—from what she tells me, nothing is good enough for your daughter. The minute she realized that Lorna resented rinsing out a cup, she absolutely forbid her to touch anything. She had to be on her toes to please your...your daughter. Apparently Lorna was more trouble than a help."

Sara did not bother to respond. She found it demeaning to get into arguments with Bessy. "I'm busy right now," she said, trying to cut off the conversation.

"Well, I won't be sending her out to more jobs so fast," said Bessy. "We certainly get gratitude for that! We try to help, and what happens? We're accused of doing things for our own benefit. I'll tell you frankly, if Melvin Kaplan finds out what happened at the Wolfsons, you couldn't blame him if he stops seeing your daughter."

ooooo

Mrs. Krinsky kept tabs on Libka through Bessy, pretending to be concerned over her welfare, but she hoped that Melvin would lose interest. She was worried about her daughter, who attended every singles function at the temple and came home lamenting, "I'm just a wallflower."

At the Sisterhood meeting Mrs. Krinsky approached Mrs. Wolfson. "Bessy Marcus tells me her niece is babysitting for your children. How is it working out?"

Mrs. Wolfson was disturbed by this question because she preferred to keep the matter quiet. She had once caught her husband peering beneath Libka's skirt when she bent down to pick up the children's toys.

"It didn't work out," she told Mrs. Krinsky. "She couldn't handle the children."

"It was nice of you to give the girl a chance. The family can certainly use the help."

"I did my best. Their smaller children used to come to my house, and they were always dirty and hungry."

"Odd family. I could never understand why Mrs. Klein introduced this girl to her nephew. He could have his pick of American girls."

Mrs. Krinsky could not control her tongue and rumours spread that Libka was guilty of things that nice girls did not do. And this reached Melvin's aunt. Mrs. Klein was a discreet woman and she found herself at a loss as to what to do. Melvin was already twenty-seven and had not been lucky in personal relationships. His parents had even mentioned that he appeared to be serious about Libka.

At a Sisterhood meeting one afternoon Mrs. Krinsky approached Mrs. Klein.

"I understand you introduced your nephew Melvin to that Hoffman girl. Are they still keeping company?"

"I believe so."

"I'm so glad to hear that."

"Well, Melvin is established in the family business and he's a homebody. He's even thinking of building in Somerhill, where the family owns land."

"I understand there's a community of young couples developing in the area," commented Mrs. Krinsky.

That evening she spoke to her daughter. "The nicest men have a hard time finding a suitable match. He's a man with serious intentions and he took you out twice. Why are you hiding? Let's find a dignified way to bring the two of you together again. After all, a girl has to show a little interest!"

Mrs. Krinsky decided to sponsor a dinner party and invite Melvin. In sending the announcement to a dozen couples, she indicated the fortieth wedding anniversary of her sister as the reason for the celebration.

Extensive renovations were undertaken in the Krinsky tenement in preparation for the event. During Fanny's previous dates with Melvin, she had not invited him inside due to the cracked linoleum on the staircase and the shabbiness in their quarters. Mrs. Krinsky now trotted into Melvin's family hardware store and ordered the best quality wallpaper for the living room. She hired a professional contractor for the job—a firm recommended by Melvin's father—and chose a kosher caterer specializing in Bar Mitzvahs and weddings.

"The tables will be turned around," she told Fanny. "You'll get the man, not that little immigrant girl."

SIXTEEN

Libka was relieving Golda in the laundromat one Saturday afternoon. The instant she walked in the door she heard the usual dialogue.

"But, lady, you said it wouldn't run," a straggly woman was saying as she held out an old spread.

"I'm sorry," Sara replied, "I can't inspect every item so personally."

"Dere's a pillowcase and my husband's new shorts missing from my wash," came from another.

"Well, if you put it in the machine it should be there."

"But you mix 'em up. Maybe you put other stuff in with my wash."

"No," said Sara, "that I don't do."

"Then how come I find somebody else's stuff in my wash the week before last?"

Sara shrugged, mumbled a few words to herself, and went to the heaps stacked on tables along the side. Carefully she pinned identification card numbers on each bag, her low mumblings lost in the hiss and swirl of the dozen machines—turning, splashing, spinning, thumping, clanging from buttons as they twirled around. Sweat was trickling down Sara's face and neck and her thin hair was damp. As customers came in, making special requests and complaints, she nodded courteously to them.

"I want this by three o'clock. Okay?"

"Okay."

"There's a blue towel in my white wash," said another. "It won't run, will it?"

"I can't promise."

"What time you closing today?"

"Six o'clock. Usual time."

"I have a few blankets. You think they'll come out good?"

"I can't guarantee."

"Did you by any chance find a baby's playsuit – red and green checkers?"

"There in the back is a pile of lost goods. You can look."

Libka emptied the smelly laundry into the machines, trying not to breathe as she did so. She took care to attach the appropriate laundry bag to each machine, with the number that corresponded to the one given the customer. The minute a washing machine stopped, she lifted the contents into a huge basket and carried it to the large dryers that stood like kings toward the rear. Transferring the damp articles, she closed the dryer door and watched through the glass window as they began to do their mad dance.

"Please fold up nice from this machine," Sara told her as she hurried by to greet a new customer who had entered with a baby carriage and two howling children.

Libka knew the machine must contain articles from one of Sara's good customers—those who did not complain but complimented her on what a fine business she ran, what reliable service she gave.

"That is Mrs. Rideau's wash—the nice French lady that teach high school. Fold up nice, please, Libkala."

"But it's not fair," said Libka. "If you fold one person's, you should fold them all."

"Don't tell me how to run."

"But if people will see you folding, they'll expect theirs to be done too. Didn't a lady ask the other day if you do folding?"

"*Sha!* You come in only to criticize. With Golda, she just work quiet and..."

Libka was transferring a heap to the dryer when she noticed a dark form enter the door. The figure was small, squat, shrouded in black netting. She moved slowly on heavy black legs, wavering from side to side.

"Who's that?" asked Libka.

Sara darted a look, then began to shake out a sheet, mumbling to herself in Yiddish.

"What?"

"Never mind."

She continued to shake sheets, ignoring the black form that stood near the door with a small brown bag in her hand.

"Aren't you going to attend to her?" asked Libka.

"She can wait."

Libka eyed her mother, aghast. Darting a look toward the door, she noticed that the black form had settled on the window ledge and gone into a strange trance.

"Is she a customer?"

"Huh? I can't hear."

The machines were spinning and clattering, the steam was hissing, and Sara was damp and drained. "*Sha!* I can't hear you talk with the machines."

Libka went over to her and shouted, "I know you're deaf but watch my lips."

"Go home already!"

"This lady," fumed Libka, "who the hell is she?"

"Go ask."

"Are you going to let her just sit in the window?"

As new customers entered, Sara was forced to go to the front, and eventually Libka saw her talking to the woman shrouded in black. She was curt, nodding her head sharply; and after taking her small brown bag and giving her a ticket to match the one she pinned on the bag, she said, "Come please back in about two hours."

Libka didn't hear the woman's reply but she was surprised to see a big smile form on her face, which was met by indifference from Sara. The woman made no move to leave and arranged herself comfortably in the window.

"Will you tell me who she is?" Libka confronted her mother the minute she approached the dryers.

"She know you are watching. Not now."

"But why are you so rude to her?"

Libka was magnetized by this strange black form. No matter how brusquely Sara treated her, the serenity did not leave her. For the rest of the afternoon she sat motionless, her eyes fixed on everything around her. She watched with a silent knowledge and dignity as the squawking customers came in, wearing house dresses or pedal pushers and sneakers with socks sucked into them. Some darted a frightened eye at her, but she seemed only to look through them in return. The aura she projected was powerful, and Libka knew that Sara was afraid of her.

"Who's that woman?" Libka asked again that night as her mother served supper.

"What you want from me? What you attracted so much to the madwoman?"

"Is she mad?"

"Two, three times a week she come in with her few torn pieces and she sit in the window and watch for hours and hours. Customers, they look funny at her. Many ask who she is. I tell her to come back later, but who know if she even hear."

"Whose laundry does she bring three times a week?"

"A few rags. And they smell bad. I don't even like to touch. Ugh! Leave me alone. Don't question me."

"But who is she?"

"I can't tell you her life history. What you want—a report?"

"Where does she come from?"

When Sara knew that Libka would not give up, she finally settled down with a cup of tea. "Somebody tell me that she is, what you call it, a fortune-teller lady. Who know? She live in a tenement in the Portuguese district and they say she is not right in the head. Of course she is not right in the head—to come and sit in the window and watch. And always in the black, with the nets and veils. Ugh! It really even frighten me!"

Libka was intrigued by her mother's words; and Golda could not understand when Libka volunteered to replace her several times at the laundromat in exchange for taking care of the younger children. The woman began to recognize Libka and a link was forming. Libka was not even surprised when one day, while Sara was in the rear by the dryers, the woman gestured to her. From a small linen sack, which was drawn together with strings, she removed a yellow card and handed it to Libka. Printed on it were the words: *Troubled? Lovelorn? Your future told by Katarina.*

ooooo

In a daring mood, Libka applied to Cambridge University. She had gone to the guidance counsellor at Little Falls High to explore this. After checking her grades, the dignified, silver-haired Miss Lee encouraged Libka. "In particular, your English teacher, Miss Murphy, feels you have much potential. I realize there are financial considerations, but perhaps a scholarship will be possible. Let's set an application in motion."

"Libkala, if you would get a scholarship to Cambridge University," Sara said, "I would let you go."

"And what about you and the rest of the family, Mom?"

"We will see. We can't run away all the time—from Lithuania to South Africa to America..."

"But I know you're disillusioned."

"We are still new in the country. Time will tell."

Libka swore her mother to secrecy, forbidding her to disclose this to her uncle and aunt, for she felt they could cast an evil spell.

It was not that she longed to study at Cambridge. She yearned to go to England so that she might see Sayyed bin Noor again. As she moved through the streets, she often imagined she saw his gentle face with the dreamy grey eyes and recalled that summer at Three Anchor Bay where he sat on the rocks and looked out to sea, and the day she found the courage to approach him.

When she wrote Anya that she was applying to Cambridge, her friend responded, *That's so exciting, Libka. I'm sure Sayyed will be thrilled too. We'll keep our fingers crossed that you'll be accepted. Did you ever believe that we could be together again?*

Libka recalled the day she came to Anya's house as she prepared to move to England. Anya was working at an ice cream parlour and her mother was taking in sewing to raise the funds for the ocean voyage. The door to Anya's room was open and the gramophone was playing "There'll Be Bluebirds over the White Cliffs of Dover."

When she saw Libka, Anya hopped up, grabbed her friend and twirled her around as she sang:

> There'll be bluebirds over
> The white cliffs of Dover,
> Tomorrow, just you wait and see.
> There'll be love and laughter
> And peace ever after,
> Tomorrow, when the world is free...

By the way, Anya now wrote, *thanks to you, Sayyed took me to lunch again near the Oxford campus. He's so impressive, Libka, so gentle and philosophical. To think that in Cape Town he could not mingle with the whites!*

Anya mentioned that she had become increasingly involved in the struggle for racial equality. *Sayyed has personalized it for me. I will devote the rest of my life fighting for the cause.*

SEVENTEEN

One afternoon as Libka approached the house, she was surprised to see her uncle's Cadillac parked in front. She was holding Dina, for the child still felt strange being left with the new family, the Schneiders, and would clutch at Libka the moment she came to pick her up. Shneyer was walking quietly at her side, mumbling the new things he was learning at school.

Libka hesitated at the front steps, wondering whether she should go in. Since the family confrontations, Meyer and Bessy seldom visited. What would they be doing at her house on a Monday in broad daylight?

A spasm of fear passed through her and she moved to the rear of the house and sneaked into the kitchen.

Hearing Sara's voice, Dina raced into the living room, Shneyer meandering behind. Then Libka had no recourse but to follow.

Meyer was sitting in his usual armchair, his head lowered. On the couch opposite him sat Sara, her eyes like dark caves. A blue airmail letter lay on the coffee table before her.

"Oy, children. Back home from school already?"

Sara drew Dina close. "My poor baby, are you hungry?"

"I'm hungry, Mama," said Shneyer. "Can I have some ice cream?"

"In a minute, darling. I will feed everybody."

Dina propped herself on Sara's lap and Shneyer sat down at her side, looking bashfully at Uncle Meyer. Libka remained standing, not sure what she should do.

"We received today a letter from Russia," Uncle Meyer addressed Libka, pointing to the blue sheet. "Sad news. Your mother will tell you."

"Yes, Libkala. Later we will talk."

Libka slipped out of the living room and tiptoed upstairs to her room. Except for an occasional sound from Dina or Shneyer, there was silence downstairs.

It was over an hour before she heard footsteps on the porch, and she watched through a slit in the blind as her uncle dragged down the steps toward his car with unsteady movements.

"What's wrong?" Libka was at her mother's side the moment the car pulled away.

"It is a tragic story." Sara's eyes were filled with an unnatural brightness. "Meyer came to the laundromat to bring the news and he drove me home. Eliahu, our youngest brother, he drowned."

"Your favourite brother?"

"Imagine! He survived the war by working as a doctor in Russia, and at last when he found a little peace..." She removed her glasses and mopped at her damp eyes. "Uh! The family was vacationing. Their adopted little girl, whose mother and father were killed in the war, ran into the sea and Eli jumped in to save her."

"Was she saved?"

"Yes, but they couldn't save Eliahu. The strong waves washed him away."

ooooo

That night, careful not to awaken Dina who slept soundly in the cot, Sara reached under her bed and pulled out a wooden chest crafted by her grandfather. It contained old coins, mementos and Yosef's medals for feats in the Black Sea as well as the treasured letters she had brought to America. Retrieving a blue envelope, she read the Hebrew letter she received from Meyer that changed the family's destiny:

> *My dear sister,*
> *At last we know the fate of our beloved family. Only our*

dear Eliahu survived, and it is from him that I have received the news. Eliahu survived because he and his wife Hinda worked as doctors in Russia. Before they left Kovna, they went to Butrimantz and begged Mother and Shleymi and his family to run away with them deep into the forest. Mother said she was too old to run, and Shleymi refused to leave Mother behind. Thus they met their fate in mass graves.

My dear sister, our family has become so small and it is important that we join together to give each other strength. Now that you have lost your dear Yosef, please prepare to come to America. Your children will be better off here, and you will all be less lonely. The tragedy that has befallen our people should remind us that we must value each other and our family.

I enclose Eliahu's letter so you can read the whole story.

For several days after hearing of the drowning of her brother, Sara moved with a strange silence and dignity. The children were careful to be considerate. Only Dina seemed more frivolous than ever. In the midst of a mournful mood she would burst into laughter and pull up her dress to reveal her bare behind.

"She's bad," Shneyer would say. "She shouldn't be laughing now, should she?"

Shneyer didn't quite know the story, but he had heard the word "dead" again and that evoked a certain memory. He would vanish for hours, and on one occasion Libka found him by the woods behind the garage, twisting a piece of string.

"What are you doing here?"

"Just thinking," he replied solemnly.

"We've been looking for you for hours. Your supper's cold."

"I don't like to eat when I'm thinking."

"Well, have you finished thinking now?"

"Yes," he replied and followed Libka into the house.

The tragedy of Sara's brother drew the family closer, and even Meyer and Bessy were less critical. They would no longer make the tour to inspect the condition of the house. They'd enter through the kitchen, Bessy putting down a jar of gefilte fish and some honey cake, then patter into the living room. They would sit in silence with Sara, their hands clasped, heads lowered. Then Libka would watch through the blinds as they shuffled toward their car.

"At least something worthwhile came out of it," she said. "Uncle Meyer and Bessy seem more human."

"It makes a person think," said Sara. "Even Meyer said the other day: 'What is the use to fight when life is so short?'"

EIGHTEEN

One Saturday night, while dining at the Stardust Lounge nestled on the highway toward Providence, Libka became aware of a familiar form through the smoke and haze. She recognized the ruddy face of her cousin. However, the noise and dancing on the shiny floor and the scuttle of waiters weaving around tables obscured her vision and clouded her mind. Could it be Ronny? What would he be doing at this lounge on a Saturday night?

She had seen him only a few times since coming to America. He was busy, his parents always said, but Libka knew that he tended to avoid contact with his immigrant relatives. He mingled with his friends from private school and worked at being seen in the right places.

Through the haze Libka became aware that Melvin was addressing her, the waiter standing over her head.

"I'm having another Highball," Melvin was saying. "Do you want a refill of your ginger ale?"

"No, thank you." She looked down at her half-filled glass.

After dancing a few rounds with Melvin, tripping over his feet as usual while he pretended not to notice, she came back to the table flustered. Just as she sat down, her eyes fell again on the ruddy face and this time she was sure it was looking at her. Still, the commotion and haziness of the setting soon dispelled the thought. Feeling that she was drifting, Melvin took her hand across the table, as he tended to do lately, and spoke of the prosperity of the family hardware business.

"Hey!" The exclamation was so buoyant that it hardly seemed like Melvin's. "Look, isn't that your cousin Ronny walking down that aisle?"

Before Libka had a chance to answer, Melvin had left the table and was heading for the squat figure she now clearly recognized. Uneasily, she sipped her ginger ale through the straw, her eyes fixed on the red tablecloth. But her ears soon filled with voices, familiar voices, and a hand stretched out toward her. "Well, Lorna, fancy seeing you here."

"Wasn't that something?" said Melvin. "I noticed him right across the floor on the other end."

How did he manage to get to the other end? Libka wondered. He must have crept to the opposite side to avoid passing her table.

"Hello, Ronny." She looked up and smiled.

Another figure stepped forward, a grey-haired man in a double-breasted suit and tie.

"Oh," said Ronny, "I'd like you to meet Mr. Brownstone. Mr. Brownstone, this is Melvin Kaplan and this is Lorna."

"Very pleased to meet you. Indeed, indeed," said the man as he shook Melvin's hand vigorously and then reached for Libka's. "Fabulous roast beef here—be sure to try it. The most superior cuts in the area by far. Enjoying the evening?" His eyes fell on Libka, who felt self-conscious in her strapless dress.

"Yes," she smiled, "it's lovely."

He cocked an ear in her direction. "Again? Again, please."

Perhaps he is deaf, thought Libka.

"I mentioned that it was lovely," she repeated a little louder.

"Aha!" Mr. Brownstone came forward and stooped down at the table between Libka and Melvin. "Is that an accent I detect?"

Libka smiled. "I only have to say one word and people ask me that."

Excitement coloured Mr. Brownstone's face as he gestured to Ronny, who seemed distracted. "Come over here, son," he said. "Have you actually heard this girl talk?" He thrust an arm around Ronny's shoulder and drew him forward.

Ronny looked muddled and annoyed. "Yes, as a matter of fact,

Mr. Brownstone, I have."

"And how he has!" broke in Melvin. "They're cousins! First cousins!"

At Melvin's words, Libka felt Ronny shrink away.

"She's from South Africa," continued Melvin. "That's where her accent is from. It is kinda cute, isn't it?"

"Cute?" said Mr. Brownstone. "Dazzling is more like it." He looked from Libka to Ronny. "Do you mean you two are cousins?"

"Yes," Ronny said graciously, "we happen to be related."

"Ronny Marcus, you come to me to be tutored in elocution when you have here before you a charming young lady who speaks the King's English!"

Ronny shrugged, and in his awkwardness his face and body seemed to merge into a shapeless heap.

"Tell me something," Mr. Brownstone continued briskly. "Can you hear me? It's rather noisy here, isn't it? Tell me," he repeated, directing his words at Ronny, "where did this girl receive her schooling?"

"She's from South Africa." Again Melvin asserted himself. "She has an African accent."

"Ah!" Something registered in Mr. Brownstone's mind as he asked, "She must be a member of the family I read about in the *Little Falls Chronicle!*"

"That's it," said Melvin. "You've hit it right on the nose, Mr... Mr... What did you say your name was?"

"Brownstone." He bowed slightly. "Calvin Brownstone." He cast an eye at Ronny who was shuffling away. "Would there be any possibility of our joining these people for a quick...coke... Hah hah hah...."

Libka caught his gaping mouth and shuddered inwardly. What a rowdy man, and he was obviously drunk.

"Mr. Brownstone," said Ronny, "if it were not for the fact that my parents are expecting me home soon, I'd be more than happy to...oblige. However..."

"Very well, very well," said Mr. Brownstone. "Hah hah hah... Well, folks, it's sure been a pleasure."

As he again extended a hand to Melvin, Libka squirmed, then she felt the tainted breath on her.

"Little miss, give your cousin a few speech lessons, will you? Now, of course, that is likely to eat into my profits... Hah hah hah...."

"He's a really nice man," Melvin remarked as the twosome shuffled toward the exit, exclaiming to many a table as they bumped along. "And you know something else..." He took Libka's hand in his damp one. "What he said about you is true, it really is."

"Pardon?" Libka eased her hand out of his as she sipped her ginger ale.

"You know, Lorna..." A pensive tone crept into his voice as he rested his elbow on the table and cradled his chin in his hand. "He really hit the nail on the head. You really do speak the King's English, don't you?"

Libka shrugged.

"Lorna, maybe I've never told you this but I'm proud to go out with you. Did you know this?" He looked at her lowered head, and she knew that his passion was mounting. "And that's the truth. You've got class...that's what it really is. Class. Don't you think so?"

Libka sipped through her straw.

"Well, let me tell you, I think you've got class—and believe me, I know. These girls you meet in Little Falls, they don't have class. You know what I mean? Tell me something, Lorna, do you think I have class?"

Again she drew a sip through the straw, aware that there was only ice left in her glass.

"Just one little weenie bit of class?"

"I guess," she mumbled.

"You mean it now—you really mean it? Or are you just saying it to make me feel good?"

She shook her head, avoiding his eyes.

"I don't say I'm such high class, but I have it over a lot of people. I mean, I didn't go to Harvard or anything like that, but did I tell you I'm a graduate of Bryant Technical Institute? Yes, two years solid business administration. Like I say, it isn't Harvard, but still.

You know what I mean? And I'm doing okay. I'm not a millionaire or anything like that, but I'm comfortable, touch wood."

ooooo

Melvin did not inform Libka of the invitation from the Krinskys, but he had no intention of going without her. After work one night, he went into his den and took out a sheet of his company stationery.

Dear Mrs. Krinsky, I would like to express my thanks for your very kind invitation to your dinner party. I would be delighted to attend and ask if I may bring along my girlfriend, Libka Hoffman, of whose family I believe you are aware. They are the relatives of Mr. and Mrs. Meyer Marcus, recently honoured by Temple Emmanuel for sponsoring this family to America...

Melvin's letter threw Mrs. Krinsky and Fanny into a dilemma and an argument erupted.

"Stop interfering in my life," Fanny wailed.

"You want to spend your whole life spinning the wheels in the mill?"

"If Melvin doesn't want me, that's not my fault."

"He wants you, but you have to show interest. Maybe he doesn't have the confidence to ask you out. Whatever's going on between him and that African girl won't last long, mark my words."

Daily fights broke out in the Krinsky household until Fanny declared one night, "I'm moving out."

But where could she go? She had lived in that tenement with her mother all her life. The world beyond her mother's tenement was bewildering to her. But in a desperate moment one Saturday she threw some articles in a suitcase and stomped out.

When Fanny did not come home that night, Mrs. Krinsky feared she might do something drastic; but if she called the police, word would soon be out in Little Falls. Though she was not inclined to pray, she took out a Bible for comfort.

When Fanny returned two nights later, Mrs. Krinsky believed G-d had responded. They fell into each other's arms and wept.

"I'll tell you, my child," Mrs. Krinsky said, "I'm cancelling that dinner party. It's too stressful. We will find another way to set things right."

NINETEEN

Libka looked up from the bag of laundry she was sorting to see a short, shapely girl with fuzzy black hair wheel a baby carriage into the laundromat.

"Hi there! How are you today?" the girl called in a loud, friendly voice.

On top of the baby lay a huge bag of laundry. The girl was smiling at Libka, her cheeks rosy, her nose freckled.

"Who are you?" she asked. "Do you work here?"

"It's my mother's place."

"You're kidding! Well, so now I've met another member of the Hoffman family! I know your mother. I adore her—such a sweet lady, so hard-working and smart. And I know your sister Gail—adorable, so refined. And you are what—the one after Gail?"

"I'm before."

"You're older than Gail?"

Libka nodded.

"How old are you?"

"Sixteen."

Libka felt herself being enveloped by the girl's arms. "You're my size. Do you mind being little? Let's measure."

Sara approached from the rear just as Libka and the girl were standing back to back.

"Mrs. Hoffman," the girl called, "you're even littler, but stand on your toes and see who's taller."

"Ugh, what is the difference?" Sara tried to dismiss the issue.

"Please, Mrs. Hoffman. Please!"

"The baby is climbing out of the carriage," Sara remarked. "Don't let her fall again." The plump, dark-skinned child seemed as vivacious as her mother.

"So this is your other daughter, Mrs. Hoffman. Now I know three in the family. And I have yet to meet the two boys and the baby, right?"

"You want me to take the laundry?" Sara asked.

"That's okay, I'll do it myself. I rinsed over the diapers beforehand, but even so, Mrs. Hoffman, I don't want you handling this stuff. Do you have a free machine?"

Sara watched as she unloaded the bag. "Be careful you don't overstuff the machines. The last time my son had to come and fix it."

"No, Mrs. Hoffman. I wouldn't want to risk breaking your machines again."

Sara observed skeptically as the girl loaded the washer. "You take out the pins?"

"Yes, Mrs. Hoffman, I remembered this time. Oh, look who's here!" The baby was waddling toward her, laughing and falling and getting up again. "Easy there, Antoinette, easy..."

When the machine was twirling, the girl looked up bright eyed and gathered the baby in her arms. Through the corner of her eye Libka saw her approach.

"So how d'you like working for your mom? What's your name? I'm Rebecca. Rebecca Medeiros."

ooooo

"Who is she anyway?" Libka asked at supper that night.

"Ugh," said Sara, "a scatterbrain. A Jewish girl married to a Portuguese."

"Oh, that's why the baby is so dark," said Libka. "She's very nice."

"A wild girl, mixed up. And she talk so open, so plain. In a few minutes you know her whole life story."

Libka decided that the laundromat was not such a boring place.

She had met that fortune-teller and now this girl. Slowly, she managed to extract more information. It appeared the girl had become pregnant while in high school, and the baby was born before she married the Portuguese boy.

As Libka continued to question her mother, Sara retorted, "You don't want to know from nice people, only the gypsies and bums."

"What do you mean, gypsies and bums?"

"Well, the fortune-teller lady, the mad one, you want to know every detail. And now you find a new friend."

To Golda's relief, Libka began to replace her more often in the laundromat. The next time Rebecca saw Libka she hugged her, and Libka found herself responding.

"Hello, twinny," Rebecca shouted. "I feel we're sisters, don't you? I like you. How do you explain that?"

Rebecca could not stop singing Sara's praises. "I love your mother. The poor thing works so hard. Imagine being stuck a widow with five small children. We used to talk a lot, but then I began to gab with my big mouth, and I think now she kinda thinks I'm an oddball, which I am. You see, I'm Jewish. My parents are Jewish—Bernstein the name is. But I'm married to a Portuguese fellow named Manny Medeiros. He's a real doll—married me after I got pregnant. The baby was already born. I shoot off my mouth and sometimes I shock people. Maybe it kind of turned your mother off. I probably shouldn't be living in Little Falls—you can't get away with much in this town—but Manny has his whole family here, seven brothers and parents who came from the Azores. My parents are old and live in the poor section of town, not where the rich Jewish mill owners are on Lakeview Avenue, like your relatives. We never did fit in with the Jewish community. So whose business is this? My brothers left, one by one. Izzy is in New York, a jazz musician, struggling. Rob is on the West Coast—he's into photography. Mark is the respectable one. He wears a white shirt and tie and is an important lawyer in Washington, married to a society woman. We never hear from him. And my favourite one, Eddie, poor Eddie, he's really far out, in a hospital in upstate New York—mental problems, you know. But he's so beautiful, writes poems that tear me apart. I haven't seen him in years...."

Rebecca looked solemnly at Libka. "You know, I like you. I really like you. Do you think I'm a nut?"

"Not really."

"What do you think of this town? I read that article about your family in the paper. When I mentioned it to your mom, she didn't want to talk about it. I even had the feeling she was sorry you people came to Little Falls."

Libka shrugged. "It's not the most exciting place."

"You go to high school?"

Libka nodded.

"I dropped out in my junior year. That's when I got pregnant and I was expelled."

For some reason puzzling to her, Libka felt drawn to Rebecca Medeiros.

"Do you think we could get together sometime?" Rebecca asked. "My place is a real rat hole. Manny is a doll but he struggles— mechanic at the gas station on Pleasant at Elm and lotsa times there's no work. But I love my place. I'd like to invite you for tea sometime."

TWENTY

After the encounter with Ronny Marcus and Mr. Brownstone, Melvin seemed more intent on displaying Libka. He was proud of the impression she had made on this elocution tutor.

"You know something," he said on their next date, "I just realized something. We always go solitaire, if you know what I mean. How about doubling up with some of my buddies? Would you like that? Can I set something up for next Saturday night? Yeah?"

The next Saturday it was not Melvin's Dodge that pulled up before Libka's house. The car that slid up was a Lincoln Continental that made Libka tremble when she peeked through the blinds.

"Ma," she shouted, "whose car is that in front of our house?"

But before her mother could enter the room, Libka knew the answer. She had glimpsed Melvin's shiny scalp.

"I borrowed my dad's Lincoln," he announced as he held the car door open for her. "A change once in a while doesn't hurt, does it?"

He took her to Somerhill, where they were invited for dinner at Melvin's closest friends, Joanie and Jason Goldberg.

"Well, Lorna!" exclaimed Joanie, a brassy blonde who fluttered about. "We're so happy to meet you at last. Do come in! And don't mind all these things lying around—maid's day off, you know."

Libka stepped onto the shiny new floor and looked around the huge rooms with the scant furniture.

"As you'll see," Joanie said, "Jason and I just moved in. How long ago is it, honey?"

A short, dark-haired man had appeared and the first thing that struck Libka was the roll of flesh around his waist.

"How long ago, honey?" she asked, smooching him.

"You're the one that counts the days," he answered, and this gave him and Melvin an exchange of laughter.

"Oh, you just don't want to admit it," she teased. "Jason honey, who do you think this is?"

"How do I know," said Jason, "with all the beautiful girls Mel escorts around town?"

"He's only teasing," said Joanie. "Honey, you know who this is."

"Of course I do," the man said warmly, extending a hand to Libka. "None other than Lorna. How do you do, Lorna? We really have been eager to meet you."

"Come, honey, follow me," Joanie intervened, "and I'll show you around. Let the boys go off and gossip, what do we care!" She stuck out her tongue playfully at Jason, then took Libka's hand and led her away.

She was shown room after room. "This here will be the baby's room—touch wood—I'm three months gone. As you can see, we haven't furnished it yet, but there's time... This is an extra room, for overnight guests. I've ordered a gorgeous queen-sized bed, and I'm doing this room up all in yellow and orange. Everything in yellow and orange, with just a little sprinkling of gold. I've ordered the rug—ooh, don't tell Jason, four hundred dollars!... This, as you see, is our dining room—the chandeliers are yet to come and a set of crystal for the cabinet display. Ooh, every time I think of it my mouth waters! I've got this thing about china and silver and crystal...."

Libka caught a glare and saw the huge rock on the girl's finger.

"Actually, Jason loves it too, but you know how men are."

When Joanie had given Libka the tour, they joined the men in the parlour where a tray of hors d'oeuvres was set up. Now Joanie and Jason spoke of their dreams, motioning through the glass walls to the vast expanse of land that surrounded their home. "I've just bought the lumber rights," Jason was saying. "We're planning to clear the area and do some construction."

"Are you going to tell them what?" Joanie asked mysteriously. "Can I?"

"You wouldn't give me a chance anyway," he said, knowing it would bring a kiss from her.

"Okay," she said, cuddling behind him. "A tennis court...swimming pool...golf course... Yes, honey?"

"Is that all? Women—they think of everything except the essentials."

"Oh, the essentials! And a four-car garage.... Is that what you mean by essentials, honey?"

As Jason leaned forward and spilled some hors d'oeuvres into his mouth, she said, "Oh, he's such a tease." She turned to Libka. "You can't take these guys seriously. I know what the others want, but what are you drinking, honey?"

As Libka hesitated, she said, "You name it, honey, we got it."

"I think I'll just have ginger ale."

"What, honey? Doesn't she have an adorable little voice?"

"She'd like some ginger ale," said Melvin. "As you can see, she's a real tough broad."

They all laughed, and saying, "Are you sure?" Joanie ran off to get the drinks.

Displayed before them on a large silver tray were a variety of spreads, shimmering black olives and a crystal bowl with shrimp. Smaller bowls contained red sauces, celery on ice, butter on ice, and a bowl of a black beady substance.

"Try the caviar before the men devour it," said Joanie. "It's delish!"

"Go on," said Jason, "don't be bashful." He pushed two dishes before her.

The thick white substance must be the caviar, she thought, as she took a slice of pumpernickel bread and spread a little on it. Then she bit into the bread and announced, "The caviar is very good."

Joanie's watery blue eyes looked stricken. "That's not the caviar, honey," the girl whispered. "That's the cream cheese."

The rest of the evening was a fog to Libka. She remembered sitting on an upholstered chair beside the table adorned with a spotless spread, candles glowing. On her lavishly painted plate a thick slice of roast beef swam in blood, and buttered string beans with walnuts were heaped on. The baked potato was wrapped in thick aluminum foil and someone was pulling it apart and filling it with sour cream. There were after-dinner liqueurs which made her feverish, and she seemed only to be aware of hands and mouths moving, but the words were a blur.

"You were terrific," declared Melvin as the Lincoln glided on the highway. "Joanie and Jason really thought you were great."

Usually he refrained from conversation while driving, but this time he overflowed with enthusiasm.

Libka could not respond, so drained by the ordeal of the evening. She felt Melvin's hand reach for hers. "I was real proud of you, Lorna. Real proud. You're such a quiet, refined girl, aren't you? Like you never lose your temper or get loud or anything like that, do you?"

She looked out of the window, feeling his sweaty hand grovel in hers.

"I really am a lucky fellow to have a girl like you."

When he reached her house, he did not park in front as he always had before, but slid the car into the driveway. He turned off the ignition. As though for comfort, Libka clutched the metal lever on her side. But then, slowly and cautiously, his hand came around behind her and drew her close. Drowsy and bewildered, she allowed it until she felt the wetness of his tongue and she broke away.

"I'm sorry," he said, "I...I couldn't help myself." He removed his glasses and she sensed his moist eyes searching her. "You don't like that?" When she did not answer, he drew her close again. "Just one last one." As he said goodnight at the door, he had an expression she had never seen before.

ooooo

It took a while for Libka to relate the severe cramps in her stomach to Melvin's double-date arrangements. Since that night with Joanie and Jason Goldberg, he was setting up something similar almost every Saturday night. Libka could not imagine where he found all these buoyant young couples, smothering each other in kisses, wandering through their partially constructed homes. They all served fancy hors d'oeuvres, and by now she was able to distinguish the cream cheese from the caviar. For dinner there would be the bloody roast beef or huge juicy lobsters that involved wearing a bib and using nutcrackers. Sometimes juice would squirt into her eye or a bone would bounce out. Then the couples would reconvene in the lounge, sip sticky liqueurs and reflect on their hopes and dreams in terms of furnishings and extensions to their home.

Rather than become more at ease, Libka withdrew further into herself. Many times she would not utter a word all evening.

"Does she talk?" a husband once asked. "I know she smiles and nibbles a little, but can she talk?"

Melvin would look at her and glow. "She's a quiet girl but honestly she talks."

When at last she would stumble into her room after the kiss in the driveway, she would free herself of the hissing dress and the girdle that dug into her flesh. Her stomach felt bloated and the stabbing pain would resume.

She was afraid to acknowledge it, for the pain was so intense. Often she would be stricken in the classroom. Nausea would sometimes accompany it, and several times she ran out of the classroom, cringing in agony in a dark corner.

When she finally told her mother, Sara did not seem too concerned. "Maybe indigestion. I will mix up a little bicarbonate of soda."

After a while Sara took it more seriously. "The heating pad. That will be the best remedy. Absolutely!"

"I think it's because of Melvin," Libka said one day.

"Don't start making dramas again!"

TWENTY-ONE

As the chill of winter settled in, Sara and Golda would come home at dark, their noses and fingertips pink from the cold.

"Uh, it is a treat," Sara would say, entering the kitchen with the customary bag of laundry. "So nice and warm in the house. A fire you make in the fireplace, Libkala?"

"What else? Would you allow us to turn on the heat?"

Dina would run to her mother and Shneyer would appear in the kitchen doorway. "My wonderful little children. I will make supper. Right away! Right away!"

She would fling off her coat and line up the potatoes and carrots. "A nice, hot, nutritious meal I plan tonight. It won't take long. Not long at all."

She would fill an aluminum pot with water and set it on the stove.

"Anybody want to help peel the potatoes and carrots?"

"Our steady diet," Libka would mumble as she reached for a sharp knife.

"I'll help." Shneyer would set himself up in a little area of his own and carve half the potato away with the skin.

As Sara worked, joyfully peeling the vegetables, Dina would stand beside her, tugging at her dress and nestling into her. "Hungry little baby," Sara would murmur. "In a minute, Dinkala, I will feed you."

When the potatoes and carrots were immersed in boiling water, Sara would lower the flame. "Now for five minutes I will go upstairs and take a little nap, then I will come down and everybody will eat. Fair enough?"

"No meat again?"

"Don't worry, Libkala, don't attack me. I figure out everything in my mind. Meat we will have."

With a mysterious look she would lift her coat and head for the stairway.

"Yes, what—those greasy leftovers rotting in the fridge?"

"*Sha!* Don't worry."

Libka had often wanted to prepare supper so her mother wouldn't have to plunge into it the minute she came home from the laundromat. But on the occasions when she did so, she realized it wasn't appreciated.

"I don't want to eat," Sara would say. "Really! Don't force me."

"How come?" Libka would eye her suspiciously. "Why, because I made a decent meal for a change? Because there's a piece of meat that costs money?"

"Everything with the money. I tell you, I am stuffed. I take an extra cheese sandwich this morning, and I eat only before I left the laundromat. Ask Golda if you don't believe."

While the children were eating, she'd be bustling at the sink, mumbling to herself.

"Huh? What did you say?" Libka would sometimes ask. "What was that?"

Sara would sense something and eye her children with an innocent smile. "Somebody say something?"

"Talking to the mice again?"

She would watch the children relish the food. "Nice meal. Libka is a wonderful housekeeper."

"Why don't you sit down and eat?"

"You know I never eat together with everybody. I will eat, don't worry."

"The leftovers, huh?"

Sara would ignore Libka's comments and return to the sink. But after the family had eaten, Libka would often watch slyly as her mother inspected the plates.

"From Beryl's leftovers alone a person can eat like a king," she would say when Libka caught her sitting down at the table. "Look for yourself—the best meat he leave, beautiful meat. If one drop of fat is on the edge, he won't touch. Besides, it is healthy a little fat, special in winter."

To this Sara would add the scraps left by Dina and Shneyer but never from Libka, whose plate would be licked clean. The only time Libka would leave food would be on the rare occasions when Beryl ate everything on his plate.

"You leave in your plate, Libka?" Sara would inquire with concern. "What is the matter—you don't feel good?"

"I'm stuffed like a pig. That's the matter."

After Sara's nap Libka would sometimes creep into the room and peek under the blanket. And as she suspected, the heating pad would still be warm. Though Sara suffered from arthritis in the damp, chilly days, she gave no sign of this.

"Using the heating pad again?" Libka would accuse.

"Why not? It is a joy to come home and lie down a few minutes with the pad. Like a queen!"

"Oh, be quiet!"

"You can also use sometimes. It isn't reserved for me."

"I don't have arthritis."

"Everything she give fancy names. If I don't complain, you don't have to worry."

Yet Libka worried about her mother. She seemed to have become so old. Sometimes she would go into her room late at night and find her lying with her eyes open, looking into space. "Aw, Libkala, you are not asleep? You got to get up early for school tomorrow."

"You have to get up before us."

"Older people don't need so much sleep."

She wondered if her mother missed Mr. Garfinkel. She recalled that last year in South Africa, how her mother had blossomed and become young when she was keeping company with him. She had even bought new outfits, wore high heels and silk stockings, and arranged her hair in an upsweep, adorning it with a glittering brooch.

Into Libka's mind flashed a scene she would remember forever. During her confinement at Kirstenhof Girls' Academy, one Sunday a prefect announced that she had visitors. She went down the spiral staircase to find her mother surrounded by her brothers and sisters. They all wore clothes she had never seen before, and she was struck at how young and pretty her mother looked. She beckoned to the man beside her, and Libka was stunned to see that it was Mr. Garfinkel. Though the notion of anyone replacing her father was intolerable, Libka found herself accepting Mr. Garfinkel's outstretched hand. As he stood among her family, he looked as young and cheerful as her mother.

They had all piled into the car and headed for Muizenberg. When her father was alive the family used to rent a summer villa there, and she would spend her school holidays diving through the balmy waters, building castles on the sand, licking ice cream from dripping cones, and hearing the pounding of the ocean at night. She would play with the Garfinkel children, listen to songs on the gramophone and cavort among the palms and cactus plants. And then on Friday night the men would arrive. Libka would wait for the sound of the car and rush off to meet her father, tumbling into his arms.

Soon after they arrived in America, there had been a number of letters from Mr. Garfinkel, and one night when Sara was downstairs Libka stole into her room and snatched a letter that had arrived from him. Though she would have murdered anyone who tampered with her mail, she could not restrain herself and was relieved that she could read the Hebrew script.

> *With continents dividing us, it is hard to maintain the flow of thought. Dear Sara, your letters reveal your disappointment in America, and I now wonder if I made enough effort to prevent your relocation. Yet what right had I to sway you from what you felt was best for you and the children? Still, when we parted at the ship I was sustained by the dream that a day may come when it would be possible for us to be together again. I*

*have been comforting myself with memories of that brief time
we had together, sitting at sunset on the terrace when the birds
seemed to trill for us alone, and that weekend with you and the
children in Muizenberg. At my age I should know that no joy
in life is forever and feel fortunate to have had such moments
to savour. No one can take that away from me. Forgive me, I
thought it was only in one's youth that one could entertain such
feelings, but perhaps in our hearts we remain young forever.*

The letters from Mr. Garfinkel were now coming rarely. Sometimes Libka would see her mother go onto the porch to check the mail and come back looking disheartened.

One evening Libka crept into the kitchen after supper. Sara had just finished washing the dishes and was drinking tea. Libka poured herself some ginger ale and sat down.

"So, Mom, you think it's good we came to America?"

"If my children are happy, it will be good."

"But what about you?"

"I already had my life."

"You're not so old, Mom. What are you?"

"Uh, leave me alone."

"You're forty-four maybe?"

"Almost forty-five."

Libka sipped her ginger ale, then asked, "Do you still hear from Mr. Garfinkel?"

"Sometimes he write."

"Is he happy in South Africa?"

Sara shrugged. "His life is also for the children. Simon is doing well in the engineering company and Shoshana is married and already have a baby."

"And Andrew?"

"He is still studying at Oxford in England. You told me he wrote to you."

"Yes, I was surprised. He wanted to know how I find life in this small American town."

"You answered him?"

"I said it's too soon to know." Then she ventured to ask, "Do you think, Mom, that Mr. Garfinkel would move from Cape Town?"

"It's not so easy to make a big change."

TWENTY-TWO

Since coming to Little Falls, the only friend Libka had made was Rebecca Medeiros. She was comfortable with her and found she could even confide in her. She told her how she felt about her dates with Melvin Kaplan and even admitted to her interest in Matt Hirsh.

Sometimes she would go over to Rebecca's tenement and take Shneyer and Dina along. The children enjoyed playing amid the broken bottles and cans, and Dina treated Antoinette like her wetting doll, dressing her up and scolding her. Rebecca also took excursions to Libka's house and would wheel her baby down the street on the metal stroller. On one occasion when Bessy was collecting for the Hadassah, she encountered this scene.

"Meyer and I found you a home on a decent Jewish street," she reprimanded Sara, "and this is what your daughter brings here. The mother doesn't belong to any Jewish organizations. No mezuzah by their door. Years ago, when I asked if they would like to donate something for Israel, she didn't have change."

One Sunday, when Libka returned with Shneyer and Dina from the Barnum and Bailey circus where she had gone with Rebecca and the baby, she found Sara sitting on the landing of the stairs, talking on the phone.

"What you mean," she was saying, "the Wolfsons made a servant out of her, so I encouraged her to leave."

Libka dashed upstairs, furtively lifting the extension phone.

"I've known Sharon Krinsky for thirty years and a false word never came out of her mouth. So you want to tell me she invented this?"

Libka listened as her aunt recounted what Mrs. Krinsky had reported. "She saw it with her own eyes—right there in the lot in front of her window: Mr. Wolfson and your daughter. Mrs. Krinsky assured me that it would only be between her and me. G-d help us that such news won't spread to Mrs. Klein and Melvin."

"I am not worried," Sara said. "Old ladies like to talk and make up stories."

"You're not worried! Can you imagine the disgrace to the whole family!"

Libka had tried to dispel the event from her mind and was horrified by Bessy's words. She had seen Mrs. Krinsky staring through her window a few times when she took a shortcut to Shneyer's school. The woman seemed to be a permanent fixture in the second-floor window of the tenement. Libka realized that the lot where Mr. Wolfson had taken her was directly below.

She knew of no way to discuss this with her mother, just as she had never been able to tell her of the encounter with Mr. Shmerl in her father's factory. She wondered what her mother thought but was relieved she did not bring up the subject.

ooooo

Perhaps the fortune-teller who sat in her mother's laundromat could shed some light on her life. "Let Katarina predict your future," read the card that Libka held in her hand. One day after school she ventured up the dark stairs to her hovel.

Now she sat in a room lit only by a red light with beads and drapes surrounding her. At a little round table before her was the strange figure shrouded in black.

"...again and again," Katarina was saying, speaking in an accent that was impossible to identify, "it shows again and again this crooked road I speak of." Her nimble fingers shuffled a deck of cards. "Many obstacles in the road...yes, many...darkness...the unknown. Many obstacles..." She cast an occasional glint of her yellow eyes on Libka.

Libka balanced on the edge of the chair, her hands clasped, clinging to every word from Katarina's lips.

"And on this dark and winding road I see the form of a man...far away...of a yellow skin. There are complications...a girl with green eyes... There's heartache, yes, heartache..."

As Libka tramped down the murky stairs from the fortune-teller's hovel, she was met with a swirling cloud of snow. It whipped her face, sent her hair flying, and she buttoned up the tweed coat her mother had bought her at a mill outlet.

She trudged through the snow, immune to the slush and mud that penetrated her shoes and the gusts beating down on her. The words of the fortune-teller flooded her mind. This man far away of yellow skin and the girl with the green eyes....

How did the fortune-teller discern the feelings she concealed from everyone? She had to talk to someone, and the next day she skipped classes and ran to see Rebecca.

"What are you doing here?" Rebecca had just put Antoinette to sleep so it was quiet in the flat. "Don't tell me you're dropping out of school too!"

"You go to my mother's laundromat all the time so you must have seen that woman in black who sits in the window for hours."

"Of course. Katarina, the fortune-teller."

"You know her?"

"I go to her whenever I have troubles. You better believe anything she says."

"Oh, that's not so good." Libka shared the fortune-teller's prophecy.

"I never told you," she said, "but I've been in love since I was fourteen."

"Libka, you're even worse than me. I got pregnant with Antoinette when I was fifteen."

Libka opened her heart and told Rebecca how she had met Sayyed bin Noor on that abandoned beach and the letters between them.

"In Cape Town I was not even allowed to talk to him because he's a Malay. When my best friend went to live in England, I told her to get in touch. And I've been so afraid that they've fallen in love."

"Hold it," said Rebecca. "You're in love with a boy you don't even know, and now you think your best friend is taking him away from you? Give me a break, Libka."

"I can't explain it, but the fortune-teller saw into my soul. And why did she say there were complications and heartache?"

Libka had hoped to get comfort from Rebecca, but her friend only shook her head and went into the kitchen and poured her a mug of tea.

TWENTY-THREE

"Tell me," Sara said as she put a dish of prune and apricot compote before Libka, "you never heard again from that boy you met at the wienie roast?"

"Why should I?"

"With Bessy's mouth you can never tell what is true, but she called earlier and told me some things."

Leave it to Bessy, thought Libka, but she was relieved that her mother wasn't asking about Mr. Wolfson. She was haunted by her aunt's disclosure about him and had tried to avoid direct encounters with her mother.

"Bessy tell me the boy Matt Hirsh is in a mental hospital in Mattapan," Sara said.

"Typical of her gossip," Libka retorted, but she began to wonder if there was any truth to it. Several weeks earlier, on prompting from Rebecca, she had broken down and phoned him. She had never imagined she could call a boy, especially someone on whom she had a crush, but after observing how Cassandra acted with her brother, she felt she should be more assertive. She recalled how alone he had been at the wienie roast and thought of the courage it must have taken to phone her. She felt she had made a poor impression on him, refusing the refreshments he offered. All she had said was "No, thank you," and it must have seemed like a rejection to him. She had hardly opened her mouth all evening and was relieved that the movies made that difficult, and then the speed of the convertible and the wind would have drowned out any words she might have uttered.

"Don't be so timid," Rebecca scolded her when she shared her disappointment that he had never called again. "A guy needs encouragement too. You talk about how Cassandra acts with your brother. Boys like it when a girl chases them. They have egos too, you know."

"So you think I should call him?"

"If you're afraid of being rejected, you'll get nowhere."

Libka decided she would take that step. One night she waited until Golda was out of the bedroom and Beryl had gone off with Cassandra. Sara was in bed with the heating pad and the younger children had drifted off to sleep.

She dialled Matt's number twice and hung up before it could ring, feeling nervous and tongue tied. On the third attempt she let it ring until someone with a fashionable accent answered, probably his mother. The woman did not ask who was calling.

When Matt came on the line, she said, "This is Lorna."

He showed no recognition of the name.

"We met at my brother's wienie roast a few months ago."

After a long silence, he said, "I've been away," as though it meant something.

It was easy for Rebecca to urge her on, but she should not have gone against her own instincts, she thought. She knew from past experience that whenever she took advice that didn't feel natural, she only made a fool of herself.

"I'm sorry I disturbed you," she mumbled. "Maybe I was really thinking of someone else. I probably dialled the wrong number."

She knew her excuse made no sense but she wanted to forget she had ever made the call. She was so humiliated that she didn't even mention this incident to Rebecca.

"It's true," her mother said, "Bessy like to gossip, but the information didn't come out of the air. Ugh, it would be a tragedy if such a boy is in a mental hospital. After all, from a distinguished family and a law student at Tufts University in Boston."

"That has nothing to do with it!" Libka fumed. She thought of that strange phone call where he showed no recollection of her. A few days later she called the hospital and was shocked to hear that the report was accurate.

"I never told you I once called him," she told Rebecca. "He didn't even know who I was."

"My brother Eddie used to have those blackouts. Sometimes I would ask him a question and he wouldn't answer until a day or two later."

"I wish I had been friendlier when he took me to the movies. I'd like to visit him."

"From what you tell me—that night at the wienie roast and your date with him—I feel something for him. Maybe it's because of Eddie in the institution in upstate New York. He's a beautiful person, Lorna. Way above anyone I've ever known. I remember the day he left home with only enough money to last him a week. He checked in at a Y in New York and probably ate at hot dog stands. My mom hasn't seen him since he left. She's so worn out that even if she had the money, she couldn't make the trip. I have dreamed of it, but there's no way I could get together that kind of dough."

As Rebecca poured tea from a burnt pot, she said, "No doubt I'm prejudiced, but if you can see Matt, I'll be real proud of you. He needs you, Lorna. He needs love."

ooooo

Libka was determined to visit Matt. The next Sunday she awoke around six and pulled over a sweater and a pleated skirt. Rebecca had given her the directions to the hospital in Mattapan.

Just as she was rinsing out her breakfast dishes, Sara came downstairs.

"So early you are all dressed up. You are going somewhere?"

"Rebecca and her husband invited me to spend the day with them. They're driving out to see friends in Maine, so I'll probably be back late."

From the terminal downtown Libka took a bus that would stop in Mattapan. She had taken along a book—*Siddhartha* by Herman Hesse—that she had read three times and now wanted to share with Matt.

A few straggly passengers crouched in the rear of the bus, and as it sped across the highway a sense of excitement flooded through Libka. This was the first time she was going off on a trip of her own in America. As she glanced through the window, her eyes devoured every sight. I'm in America, she thought, and realized what a far way she had come. Only a short time ago she had been confined at Kirstenhof Girls' Academy, where she had to wear the austere uniform and Mevrou Vandermerve put her in detention for corresponding with the Malay boy. And here she was free to wear whatever she wanted and to travel on her own.

She seemed to have drowsed off and was shaken awake as the bus lurched to a stop. What had she been dreaming? There were two men, Mr. Shmerl and Mr. Wolfson. They had dragged her into a cave and were about to do something when she awoke.

As the bus sped on, her life fleeted before her. She was back in the house in Green Point, where Maputo polished the steps and the brass plaque on the gate. The song he used to sing after her father died came back to her strong and clear:

My baas, he left the earth,
In the great heavens he now dwells.
May the good Lord, may He,
Look upon my baas
As Maputo had looked upon him...

Libka ignored the tear that dribbled down her cheek and looked out of the window at the trees covered with snow, like the silver-leaf trees beneath which she'd stroll on her way home from school.

As the bus leaped onward she felt as though she were flying. How would it feel to be in an airplane, gliding through the sky? She closed her eyes and tried to imagine. Someday I'll go on a plane. I'll go to far-off places. I wonder what Daddy would think if he saw me now, riding by myself to another city. She enjoyed the tears that came, relieved there was no one to intrude on her memories.

ooooo

When she reached the institution, she wondered what had brought her here, but she forced herself to enter the desolate lobby. The linoleum stretched endlessly in the murkiness of the hall. At the reception desk she asked the burly black figure for Matt Hirsh.

"Go on up to the third floor."

When she looked around, he pointed brusquely. "The elevators are at the green door to the left."

A chill permeated the slippery hall; the walls were a deathly grey.

When the elevator landed, a few stern nurses stepped out, and Libka cautiously entered, pressing the button marked three. As the door opened she found herself in a barren hall. A young woman with a slimy mouth gaped at her. She gurgled, then lost her balance; and as she swivelled around, Libka noticed the white legs that seemed never to have seen the sun. Her limp cotton dress was caught in her behind, and white anklets were trapped in her heavy brown shoes. As Libka moved in the direction where she sensed activity, the girl waddled after her.

Seeing a man mopping the linoleum, she asked, "Where may I find Matt Hirsh, please?"

"If he's not in the lounge, he'll be in the ward."

The faded couches and armchairs were bare of people, but in the far corner near the window Libka noticed a young woman in a blue terry robe. As she looked up, Libka was struck by her raven hair and ivory skin, and the glow of her purple eyes. The girl put her book aside and bounced up, wiggling her shapely form and smiling as she approached.

"May I help you, please?"

Surely she was not a patient, thought Libka. Perhaps she was a visitor like herself.

"I'm looking for someone called Matt Hirsh."

"Matt. Of course!" As she smiled, her high cheekbones glowed.

"Who may I say is calling?"

"I'm not sure if he'll remember me, but my name is Lorna Hoffman."

"That's lovely. Lorna. Like Lorna Doone." Smiling joyfully, she wiggled away, calling back, "I'll go fetch Matt."

During the long wait, Libka considered slipping out, wondering again why she had made this trip.

She picked up a mottled leaflet from the rack and began reading the strange pieces written by the inmates.

She heard footsteps and looked up to see the girl leading a stiff figure toward the lounge. Libka had to lower her gaze, for Matt glared with vacant eyes like those of the dead.

Libka moved tentatively toward him. "I hope you don't mind that I came to see you," she said softly.

He showed no reaction, then turned abruptly and strode off to a chair a distance away.

The girl gave Libka a sympathetic look and disappeared down the corridor.

Libka clasped the copy of *Siddhartha* she had brought along but sensed she shouldn't approach him. She found herself sinking into the limp green couch.

She pretended to concentrate on the house publication—the raw statements, the childlike drawings and verse. Matt had not shifted. Finally, she moved furtively toward him and held out the book. "I thought you might like this."

He accepted gently, read the title solemnly, then flung the book to the ground and stormed out.

Libka lifted it and took it back to the couch. A few figures wandered in, eyed her intently, then navigated back down the corridor. An ashen-faced man stared at her, then took a straight chair and glared into space. A shrivelled woman, her face scorched with deep lines, mumbled to herself. A terrified couple stumbled in with a girl who was tossing her dishevelled blond hair. A man whose eyes looked like holes in his head wheeled himself in.

Finally, Libka returned the leaflet to the rack and pulled over her coat. She had already pressed the elevator button when she sensed a presence behind her. There stood Matt, looking remorseful. "I'm sorry." Libka felt safe to proffer the copy of *Siddhartha*, and he accepted with a bow. As she swept into the elevator, she looked back and saw that his eyes were no longer glassy but soft and warm.

TWENTY-FOUR

"I've been meaning to ask you," Melvin said, "anything in particular you'd like to do New Year's Eve?"

It was only a few days into December. Libka wondered if this was the reason they had gone alone to this sedate lounge, instead of pairing off with the couples as they had been doing since that evening at the home of Joanie and Jason Goldberg. And what made him so sure, she wondered, that she would go out with him New Year's Eve?

"It doesn't matter," she said.

"What doesn't matter?" Now on his third Highball, he removed his glasses and his watery eyes looked across the table into hers.

"It makes no difference where we go," she said quickly, averting her eyes.

"Why do you always look away? Is there some reason for that?"

"I didn't realize I do it." She dared herself to look directly at him.

"That's better." His hand reached out to hers on the table. "Come on, there must be a place you really like, something a little more special."

"All the places you take me to are nice."

"You're such a well-mannered girl, did anyone ever tell you that?"

Again her eyes were lowered, but he was touched by it. "A little shy too. I think that's why you don't look at me.... Well, I have something in mind. What about the Primrose Palace in Framingham?"

"I'm sure that would be very nice."

"Ever been there?"

"No."

"They have good New York steaks and seafood...and there's a band and a big floor for dancing. Everybody gets dressed up kinda formal. I know you'll like it."

He pressed her lifeless hand. "Can I make reservations? You know, New Year's Eve and all. Okay, honey bunny?"

On rare occasions, after he had had at least two drinks, Melvin would use that endearing term. No doubt he had learned it from the couples whose unfinished homes he frequented.

"Do you realize," Melvin said after clearing his throat, "you and I have now been going together for just about six months? Remember that nice aunt of mine who fixed us up?"

Libka nodded.

"Time really flies. So tell me, Lorna, how do you think you've adjusted to Little Falls?"

"All right, I guess."

"Your modesty is so sweet. You really are an unusual girl—did anyone ever tell you that?"

"Not really."

"There you go again!" He clapped his hands and laughed. "So you'll be graduating high school in June. You never really told me what your plans are after that."

"I haven't really worked them out."

"Is there any possibility that you won't remain in Little Falls?"

"Why do you ask that?"

"A lot of young people leave this town. They complain there isn't enough excitement for them here. Well, I certainly never feel that way, do you?"

"Don't they leave in order to do things they can't do here," Libka asked, "like to go to college, for instance?"

"There're colleges around here, like the one I went to. You can major in business administration, economics—you name it! And for girls there are all kinds of good secretarial schools in Providence. Katherine Gibbs. They even have a secretarial training school right here in Little Falls."

"I see."

"Do you have some special plans, like going away to an out-of-town college or something like that?"

She wondered what he was getting at. Did he sense her thoughts?

"You didn't answer me. Some little secret up your sleeve?"

"No secret."

"Is there something that might help you make up your mind?"

When she looked at him, not understanding, he continued, "I guess we haven't had a chance to really talk, have we...always with friends around. That's why I thought it would be nice to be alone tonight. What would you think if I told you I'm planning to build a house?"

She caught a glimpse of the saliva in his mouth and had to look away.

"That's the truth," he said. "And where do you think of all places? Somerhill!" He eyed her curiously. "Remember the time we went to Joanie and Jason's? You never did tell me what you thought of their house."

"Oh, very nice."

"What do you think of my building one just like it? The land's there, waiting. Over ten acres in the heart of Somerhill...with a stream running right behind it. Good level ground—tennis court, swimming pool, the whole shmeer!"

Libka escaped into her ginger ale.

"It's hard to know," he said. "You're a funny girl. You don't show too much reaction, do you?"

As she looked at him, pretending not to understand, he continued, "Well, wouldn't any other girl squeal so loud you'd hear it all the way to Somerhill?"

Libka giggled.

"Tell me something, what does your mother think of us, or of me?"

"She has a very high opinion of you."

"Is that so? I'm complimented!" He drank. "She's a nice lady, your mother. Tell me something, she doesn't nag you too much?"

"About what?"

"Well, you know, like all Jewish mothers... She knows that you and I have been going steady now for about six months. And she doesn't pressure you...about the future and so on?"

Libka indicated not.

"I can't say my parents don't. They would like the pleasure of meeting you, but they already know the impression your family made on my aunt. And of course they think the world of your relatives. They're not surprised Temple Emmanuel honoured them for their noble deed in bringing you people over. Just yesterday my mother said, 'You're a man of twenty-seven. What are you waiting for—for all your hair to fall out?' I must admit, I don't have that far to go." He reddened more than he had expected and stroked his strands of hair to cover the bald spots.

"Would you be interested in looking the land over with me some afternoon? Maybe you have ideas about where the house should face and so on. I know women are usually very good about it."

"I'm not really an expert on such things."

"Oh, come on now, Lorna. You know a lot more than you admit. You think maybe next Saturday afternoon we could take a drive out?"

Libka acquiesced.

TWENTY-FIVE

"Damn it, he asked me out for New Year's Eve!" Libka grumbled.

Confused and ecstatic, Sara looked up at the kitchen clock. "So early? Really?" Then she ran to the newspaper on the table. "Only December five and already?"

"Make me some tea."

Sara gave Libka a joyous look before she dashed to the stove to put on the kettle. "What will you wear, Libkala? After all, New Year's Eve..."

"How come you don't ask if I plan to go?"

"All right! All right!" Sara tapped Libka's arm playfully. "I will tell you what I think. In fact, I have already for a long time in my mind, but of course only for a very special occasion. You remember the rich black velvet we buy in England when the ship stop on the way from South Africa? About four yards we got from the velvet. So I was thinking maybe to make a beautiful strapless dress with a little cape to match." Before Libka could respond, she added, "And the rose-coloured silk—a beautiful remnant. That would be ideal for a lining for the cape and by the bodice of the dress. Uh! An outfit for a princess! Of course I wouldn't sew myself. I hear of a dressmaker in Providence. Bessy go to her. She isn't cheap but for such occasions I don't look for bargains. Believe me, we can still afford."

"How come you're acting so rich?"

"All right. All right." Sara hurried to the stove, where she poured hot water over the tea leaves in the strainer.

"How many cups of tea have you already made with those few leaves?" asked Libka.

"Strong tea, I swear. Only Beryl and Golda have cups and I put in a heaping tablespoon! What you want from me? I will also have a cup of tea."

She hastened back to the table with the cups and sat down opposite Libka.

"So what do you think of Matt Hirsh?" Libka taunted her.

"Ugh! Stop already! I told you he's in a mental hospital."

"Leave it to Bessy to deliver all the good news."

"Also a tragedy what became of him. A brilliant student at Tufts University, studying to be a lawyer."

"Maybe he hated it. Maybe his rich parents drove him to a nervous breakdown."

"Ugh, we shouldn't know from such things."

"If only he would ask me out again instead of that sickening Melvin Kaplan."

Libka took a gulp of tea and sped upstairs before her mother could respond.

ooooo

When Bessy inquired whether Melvin had asked Libka out for New Year's Eve, Sara admitted that he had, though Libka was angry at her mother for revealing this.

"Maybe I won't even go!"

"*Sha!* It is something to be ashamed of? And you will look like a princess in the velvet outfit."

"Don't build up your hopes, Mom. When I get through high school, I'm leaving this town, whether I hear from Cambridge or not."

"Listen, my child, if you will hear good news from Cambridge University of course I will send you."

Though Libka had not permitted her mother to disclose anything about Cambridge to her uncle and aunt, she allowed Sara to say she planned to attend college.

"So what will she be, tell me—secretary to the president of the United States?" Meyer exclaimed when Sara mentioned this one Sunday afternoon.

Meyer looked at his wife, who was nestled on the couch beside Sara, and Bessy responded, "Imagine, university!"

"But if she can get a scholarship," said Sara, "I don't see why not."

"Scholarship," Bessy mouthed sarcastically. "That doesn't pay for everything. A girl goes away to college, she needs a wardrobe, she needs a roof over her head, she has to eat."

"And who will provide?" asked Meyer. "From your laundromat, from such a goldmine, you are going to send your children to universities?"

"Thank goodness I don't have to depend yet on the laundromat. I am satisfied if it can cover the everyday expenses in the house. After all, Meyer, you know yourself—we came to this country not poor people. Of course the house in South Africa I had to sell fast, but you will remember that Abraham Garfinkel bought the factory for his son and he gave me a very fair price."

Bessy nudged Sara with a twinkle in her eye. "You still hear from him?"

Sara resented this intrusion. "We correspond sometimes." She regretted she had ever mentioned Garfinkel to them.

"Whatever the situation," broke in Meyer, "money doesn't grow on trees. It goes. In America it goes very fast. So Libka you will send to college, Beryl you will send to college…"

"One thing I know," said Sara, "if my husband was today alive he would insist that the children have the best opportunities. I am careful not to spend too much with food, with heat. Clothes the children manage with the same. But one thing I believe: education is an investment. And Libka, after all, will graduate at sixteen, the youngest in the school, on the Dean's List, all A's… So if such a girl already don't go…"

"But tell me, Sara," Meyer said with a smirk, "so let's say she go to university. Four years she study, bury her nose in books. What happens after she graduate with the big degree?"

"Like you say, Meyer," said Bessy, "she'll become secretary to the president of the United States."

"So there you are!" declared Meyer, sitting back smugly.

"Let's be realistic," said Bessy, "what does it matter if a girl got a degree? G-d willing, if all goes well, who knows... It's possible that Melvin Kaplan may have intentions. You said he asked her out for New Year's Eve?"

"You never know," Meyer added with a chuckle. "He could have something up his sleeve."

Sara showed no reaction.

"And if she goes away to another city, another state," Bessy mused, "a man like Melvin Kaplan won't wait around forever. There are other fishes in the sea."

"Bessy has a point," said Meyer. "A girl goes away for four years, how do you know what can happen? There is an expression, 'Absence makes the heart fonder.' Well, I don't believe it. A young man, he's not a priest, he meets somebody else and things can develop. There is a right time, and a smart person knows when to recognize the time."

"Meyer's right," said Bessy. "I have to say, he's right."

"As for me," said Meyer, gesturing to his wife, "obviously I goofed up and chose the wrong time. So what did I do, I had to take what I could get."

"Oh, Meyer!" Bessy turned scarlet. "Imagine talking that way about your own wife!"

"What you want, that I should be a hypocrite? I tell you straight to your face."

As Bessy smouldered with embarrassment, Sara continued gravely. "Well, listen, Meyer and Bessy, I guess everybody got to figure out what is best for themselves. If you are so much against education, how is it that Ronny got already plans to attend Harvard University?"

"Harvard!" Bessy eyed Meyer. "Huh, what parents wouldn't be thrilled? If our son can get into Harvard, we should turn down such a chance?"

"Sara," said Meyer, "how can a woman like you ask such a question? If Bert would apply to Harvard and he would be accepted, you think we would discourage him?"

"Well, I'm not sure. Him you want altogether to go work in a factory. Maybe he like to have fun, but he was also a good student and he is interested in becoming an engineer. In that respect he take after Yosef, may he rest in peace. His hands are like magic. The machines in the laundromat break down—old machines and people stuff in all kinds of junk—but the minute Beryl come in, I can have a rested mind. One look, one touch, and it begin to spin like magic."

"He could work as an apprentice," said Bessy, "if he's really so capable."

"And I am very pleased that he already made application to a few colleges."

"It's nice to be wealthy," scoffed Bessy.

"I wouldn't dream otherwise," said Sara. "My children will have a good education."

TWENTY-SIX

"I was thinking," Melvin said the next Saturday afternoon, "how about putting your hair up for New Year's Eve?"

"Why?"

"Let's face it, wouldn't it be nice if you could get a real drink, like maybe a Grasshopper or a Pink Lady? With your hair up you'd look a little older so maybe they wouldn't bother you for identification."

They had just made a tour of his land in Somerhill and were heading back to his Dodge.

Strolling through the woods, the trees sprinkled with snow, evoked the silver-leaf trees of Libka's childhood...and the *veld* through which she used to roam. A small, makeshift hut in the distance became the haunted house where the yellow-skinned woman would press her nose against the glass and distort her mouth into a grotesque shape. What a strange day that had been, the day the gnawing occurred in her stomach and she discovered the first trace of her womanhood. She had gone back to her childhood world and the house in Newlands where the fluffy yellow chicks burst from their shells and the hedges abounded with honeysuckles.

"I hope you don't mind I told them."

Before her was the face of Melvin, grinning sheepishly. Amid the vastness of the land and against the sky, he looked even more scalped and raw.

"Mind what?"

"You mean you didn't hear?"

"I didn't get the last part," she lied.

"I told my parents that I'm taking you to see the land today."

"Oh, that's nice."

He eyed her adoringly. "Somehow you look more than ever like a little girl today...maybe it's that pinafore with the cute pink sweater. Shouldn't you button up your coat, though? Don't you feel a little chilly? I mean, especially for a hot-blooded girl from tropical Africa!" He took this chance to put his arm around her and draw her close. As she stumbled along under his clutch, he continued, "So, naturally, my parents asked if I have something in mind. I hope it's all right I told them how much you mean to me."

Libka broke away, pretending to button her coat.

"Is it okay I said that?" he asked.

"I just remembered," she stammered, "I have to take care of my sister and brother." She checked her watch. "Can you take me home now?"

The cramps had invaded her stomach, and she hugged her coat, her teeth chattering, as she stumbled toward his car.

ooooo

When Libka came home, Beryl informed her that Matt had called. "I understand he's going through a hard time, but he said he's home for the Christmas holidays. Why not give him a call?"

Libka fled upstairs and dialed his number. She would be assertive. She would be like Cassandra. Then maybe she wouldn't be stuck with someone like Melvin Kaplan.

She was relieved when Matt answered and recognized her voice.

"As I told your brother, I'm home for the holidays. If you're not busy, perhaps we can go to a movie."

"I can't think of anything better."

The fatigue that had enveloped her when surveying Melvin's land had vanished and blood seemed to rush in her veins. She lifted the phone and called Rebecca.

"Guess what? I'm going out with Matt on Christmas night."

Rebecca made an exuberant sound. "Did he call you from the hospital?"

"He's home for the holidays."

"Good for you."

"Melvin was expecting me to see him, but I'll lie and tell him relatives from New York are coming."

"If he finds out the truth, would you care?"

Libka giggled. "Maybe I could get rid of him that way."

"You don't want to be seeing that guy and all those lovey-doveys in their grand surroundings."

"I'm punishing myself by going out with him. When he showed me his land, I think I had a blackout."

"Honey, you won't be doing anyone a favour by giving in. If you married Melvin, you'd be miserable, so how could anyone around you be happy? Do you think my mother was in favour of my marrying Manny? It wasn't even that he's Portuguese and my going against my Jewish religion, but he has no education or training. But today she adores Manny and eats Antoinette up. Listen, a lot of people think I'm a dope, but I understand a bit about what really matters. Follow your heart, Lorna, and you'll never be sorry."

ooooo

Matt arrived about an hour late, but Libka was pleased. She had always cringed at Melvin's promptness. If she peered out of the window on the stroke of eight on a Saturday night, the Dodge would be pulling up, followed by the chime of the doorbell.

She felt relaxed by Matt's manner—leaping up the steps in casual attire. She too had dressed simply, in a black wool skirt and sweater with an olive pendant, and she wore her tweed coat.

"*The African Queen* is playing at the Waverly," Matt said. "Would you care to see it?"

"Very much."

He drove with a purpose, and when they entered the dark street that would take them to the main road, Matt slowed down and said, "I hope you're not going out with me due to politeness or pity."

"I was relieved when you called," Libka answered earnestly. "I wasn't sure I behaved right when I came to see you." She was surprised at the ease of her confession.

"I think you can reverse that statement, but I guess that's why I'm in the hospital."

"Did you ever read that book?" she asked.

"I had no intention of reading it, but I opened it at random and something caught my eye...and I read that page and the next one and then I realized I was pretty far into it, so I went back and read the whole thing. How did you know *Siddhartha* would mean so much to me?"

"Only because it had that affect on me."

"I think you're a sensitive girl."

When they reached the theatre, he asked if she wanted popcorn and ice cream, and this time she accepted the ice cream. Matt helped her out of her coat and removed his suede jacket. She was not altogether surprised when much later, well into the movie, his hand played around hers; but she was amazed at her courage in linking her fingers to his. She felt a warmth and shiver at the touch, and their hands remained together till the end of the movie.

Driving home, he said, "I would have liked to take you somewhere nice, but you know my situation. My pass expires by noon tomorrow, so my dad will be driving me back quite early."

Pulling up in front of Libka's house, he left the engine running. "You'll never know how much this evening has meant to me."

She wanted to tell him this was the most exhilarating evening she could remember, but words did not seem enough.

As there was no sign that he would turn to her, she eased her way out of the car. He did not move until a light came on the porch and her mother appeared in the doorway.

TWENTY-SEVEN

"You look lovely this evening."

Removing his Russian fur hat, Melvin looked clipped as a hen, his face rosy. A carnation was pinned on his coat lapel. He glanced from Libka to the others gathered in the room. "Mrs. Hoffman, your daughter looks very lovely this evening."

"Thank you, Melvin." Sara's face shone with happiness. "You look very nice also."

She turned as though to beckon the others to come forward. Slightly behind her stood Golda, Shneyer and Dina, all dressed as though they too were going to the Primrose Palace. Dina had insisted on wearing her red coat and hat to greet Melvin.

In an instant Beryl appeared on the landing. Smelling of shaving lotion and eau de cologne, he too was dressed for New Year's Eve—in a navy-blue suit, white shirt and floral tie.

"How do you do?" He took the few steps into the living room and moved briskly toward the guest. "Happy New Year!"

Flustered and festive, Melvin shook hands energetically. "May as well do the same with everyone." One by one he approached the Hoffmans, shaking each one's hand and repeating "Happy New Year!" When he came to Dina, she had both hands ready; and as he took them, everyone laughed.

The revelry was cut off by the appearance of two figures on the porch. In the confusion, no one had heard the car pull up before the house. A shiver ran through Libka as she stole a look at the mink cape in her arms—a gesture from her aunt.

"After all," Bessy had said when she made a special trip to study the black velvet outfit Libka had made for the occasion, "you don't wear a little school coat with such a dress. She did a fine job—Mrs. Hamilton—and look the rose lining how perfect she installed it. I don't know why I do this—I get no thanks—but considering the company and the occasion, I'll let her wear my mink cape."

Libka had protested, and several times afterward she told her mother she would not wear her aunt's mink cape.

"Shame on you," Sara said, "sometimes I really wonder who is right. She make a trip to look over the outfit and offer such a fancy fur."

"I don't want her favours. I'd feel ridiculous in a mink cape."

Libka knew she would give in. And when her aunt brought over the mink and Libka again tried on the outfit, this time with the mink, even her aunt looked at her in a new way. Before leaving, she asked, "What time is Melvin picking you up?"

"Around seven o'clock."

"I won't guarantee," she said to Sara, "but if Meyer and I can come by to say hello, we very well may. He's a nice boy, honourable."

ooooo

"What a pleasure to see you!"

Melvin turned to Bessy and Meyer in the doorway. "Well, if this isn't a surprise. Hello, Mrs. Marcus... Hello, Mr. Marcus..." He shook hands, the sweat glistening on his forehead.

"Now isn't this a jolly crowd!" exclaimed Bessy, looking around. "Everyone so dressed up and cheerful."

"And you look your usual radiant self, Mrs. Marcus. My, that's a stunning little coat you're wearing."

Bessy looked down at her tweed coat. "Huh huh... Imagine. I made it myself...in the sewing class."

"I'll be darned," said Beryl, stepping forward and offering his hand. "Happy New Year, Aunt Bessy."

"The same to you." She looked up at her handsome nephew.

"My, don't we look smart."

"Thank you, Aunt. Thank you." Beryl made his way to his uncle. "Happy New Year, Uncle Meyer...yes, indeed..."

"And the very same to you, Bert," remarked Meyer. "Maybe it is in order to make the rounds."

As everyone laughed and Dina tried to gain special favours, Meyer stepped from one to the other.

"A happy gathering," Sara said in a joyous tone. "Everybody laughing and cheerful." An idea popped into her head. "Beryl... Bert...maybe, uh, maybe we will offer the Manischewitz wine?"

"Good idea! Excellent thought."

Sara hurried toward the sideboard in the dining room, followed by Beryl, who first bowed and said, "If you'll kindly excuse us a moment."

Libka took the opportunity to slip out and dash into the kitchen.

Sara unloaded the mauve wine glasses from the cabinet display, carrying them into the kitchen. Beryl produced the bottle of wine.

"What is this," Libka whispered, "a celebration?"

"Why not?" Sara's face was radiant. "Even Melvin say you look lovely this evening."

"The less you compliment her, the better," Beryl said flippantly. "Hand me the glasses while I pour."

"All right, all right, my Berala."

"What business is it of Bessy's," Libka whispered, "popping in uninvited? Now she'll have something more to gossip about."

"*Sha!* They will still hear. Bring the tray to put the glasses on."

"I'm not going out with him. My stomach pains are worse than ever."

Sara and Beryl ignored her comment.

Libka lingered beside the stove, listening to the crescendo of voices, the false laughter, the empty words. The voice that cut deepest was that of Melvin. How slimy he looked tonight. And why did he have to wear that carnation on his lapel and the fur hat with the flaps at the ears?

"Libki, mibki, pibki..." Dina came bounding into the kitchen and pulled Libka into the living room. "Libki, pibki, mibki, mumki..."

Finding security in the child's company, Libka joined the group in the living room.

After a toast, the couple departed like honeymooners, the spectators waving until the car reversed and headed down the street.

"And you?" Bessy turned to Beryl. "Who's the lucky young lady?"

"A friend." Beryl smiled broadly to cover his discomfort.

"Not telling?"

"Not at all," said Beryl, "not at all, Auntie. But I have no special announcement to make."

"Is that right?" There was sarcasm in Meyer's voice. "I would say that makes one open to suspicion."

His mouth turned down in a grin and he nodded to those in the room.

"Well," said Beryl, "if you don't mind..." He backed toward the stairway.

"Tell me..." Bessy captured him. "You're taking out a girl tonight?"

"What you think, Bessy," said Meyer, "he is taking out the bloodhound next door?"

Beryl laughed, but Bessy went on. "We know the girl, the family?"

"You may," said Beryl. "As a matter of fact, you just may."

Sensing his awkwardness, Sara came to the rescue. "Somebody would like a cup of tea?"

"That's a good idea, Mom. Excellent idea. Coming in from the cold, Uncle and Aunt would surely..."

"The girl lives in the neighbourhood?" Bessy persisted.

"Pardon?" Beryl cleared his throat. "No, no, as a matter of fact, she doesn't."

"She doesn't?"

"He met her in the poolroom," said Meyer. "What you want from the fellow?"

"Huh...huh... A nice young man like that. She goes to the temple?"

Sara's voice came forward, strongly this time. "So I should make tea?"

"We just had your Manischewitz wine," squealed Bessy. "What you want from us with your tea? Listen, we like to know about the young ones. Beryl, a good-looking fellow, we like to know he's in the right company. We know from the girl's family? They belong to the temple?"

"No," Beryl said firmly, "she's not Jewish."

"Imagine that!" Bessy whimpered as Beryl leaped up the stairs. "New Year's Eve and a shiksa he takes out."

ooooo

When the group had dispersed and Shneyer and Dina had been put to bed, Sara and Golda sat in the kitchen drinking tea.

"Did Beryl take out Cassandra?" Golda asked.

"Who knows? He don't give me a report. Goldala, you want maybe a piece of strudel with the tea?"

"Okay, Mom."

"Uh, my golden child, with you is always a pleasure to deal."

Sara brought a plate of strudel to the table. As she cut it, she said cheerfully, "So only Golda and I are wallflowers, huh? No date on New Year's Eve!"

Golda smiled dreamily. "Libka looked so beautiful in that outfit, so beautiful..."

"Well, my child, you still have lots of time, but one day you will also wear such an outfit."

"How old is a girl when she can start going out with boys?"

"With every girl is different, but I don't think it's advisable too early. It is more important to do well in school. Sixteen, seventeen, maybe a girl can go on a date."

"So how come Libka's going with Melvin and she's only sixteen?"

"I would never have dreamed of such a thing. She is smart in books but socially not so developed. Who can know? Melvin apparently must be interested."

"But, Mom, she hates him so much, how can she be with him?"

"You know her already. If we would not approve, she would like him. Because we think he is a respectable man, she make like she can't stand him."

"What if he discovers she went out with Matt on Christmas night?"

"With lies is no good, special in a small town. Anyway, he looked satisfied with Libka tonight, so who knows what will be."

ooooo

As Melvin drove along the highway heading for Framingham, the radio played holiday music. He was a slow driver and on this evening proceeded more cautiously than ever. "You know how it is, holiday traffic and all."

Entering the Primrose Palace, she was overcome by the flickering coloured lights, the slippery dance floor, streamers and balloons. Men in tuxedos and bowties escorted women in satin gowns and glittering slippers, mouths like bloody hearts, hair like tinsel. The maitre d' led the couple past the crowded tables to the one reserved for them.

Libka ordered a Pink Lady and Melvin was proud she had not been questioned about her age.

"Didn't I tell you? Putting your hair up makes all the difference! And it looks lovely too, very sophisticated."

They danced on the slippery floor. Feeling dizzy from the sticky pink substance in the cocktail glass, she stumbled after him as he jerked her arm in time to the music. As each piece ended, he clapped and cheered. Not even in the days at boarding school had she felt such isolation. Couples were laughing and cheering, dancing with their bodies entwined, feasting, clowning. And before her was a man who looked upon her with adoration. Why was she consumed by such loneliness and panic?

"Come on," he said after several rounds of dancing, "drink up and let's order you another. After all, New Year's Eve!"

In a moment of abandon, Libka poured the drink down her

throat. "Delicious!" she uttered.

Delighted, Melvin signalled for the waiter. "Another round, please."

When he coaxed her into the next dance, she lost her balance. He welcomed this chance to draw her close and he twirled her around. Drowsily her head fell to his shoulder; and when he swept her into his arms, she did not recoil.

After the blackout and the commotion that ushered in the New Year, Melvin surreptitiously removed a little black box from his suit pocket. He fumbled with it, then reached for Libka's left hand and slipped a ring onto her third finger. "I hope you will give me the honour of accepting this."

She glanced down at the diamond. The blinding rock seemed lost on her childlike hand.

"It looks lovely," he said, "and I'm glad it fits."

She did not raise her eyes to meet his.

"I hope it's not too much of a surprise," he said. "I wasn't sure if I should warn you..."

She had no recourse but to look at him, and she looked directly into his eyes.

"No one has ever been as kind to me as you have. You are one of the nicest people I've met in my life." She lowered her eyes. "It's a beautiful ring."

"May you wear it in joy and happiness." His hand came over hers. "You are the girl I would like to share my dream house with."

She felt the sting of tears.

"Did you expect it at all?" he asked.

"I don't know."

"I realize you're only eighteen, and sometimes girls like to wait a little longer before they settle down, but we don't have to rush. Another six months or a year... Even if we start on the house now, it would take that long."

The words tore out of her: "I can't..."

Melvin's eyes sprung to her as she averted hers.

"I just can't..."

"You can't what?"

"No, no..." She slipped the ring off her finger and it rolled toward him. "I'm...only sixteen..." She started to cry.

"Don't cry. Please don't cry. It's been too much for you...too much of a shock..."

She did not remember the trip home, but the next morning she awoke feeling her head would split.

TWENTY-EIGHT

Libka was not confident that her application at Cambridge University would be accepted, and she had to admit to herself that her heart was not in it. She yearned to write and was encouraged that her English teacher saw promise in her work. If she went to university she would have to devote herself to subjects that would only intrude upon her true passion.

She felt she had to leave Little Falls and needed to save for a ticket. It was not only the thought of Melvin Kaplan, but the encounter with Mr. Wolfson. And then there were her relatives who made life impossible for her.

She began to seek work, and during an interview in a downtown stationery store she made a favourable impression on the owner. "We have a good clientele and your British accent is an asset," said Mr. Rabinovitz. "We'll start you at a beginner's salary and if you do well, after three months we may give you a raise."

Libka went to her job after school and worked until the store closed at six. She never hesitated to stay late if there was inventory to check or other tasks the owner required. Sometimes the last bus would pass through town and she would have to walk home.

"It looks to me that you do better without Bessy's help," Sara said proudly. "Anyway, she sent you for the wrong jobs. You are not suitable to work in a mill."

Customers had no difficulty understanding Libka's speech. Some would ask, "Are you by any chance from England? I sense a British accent." And when she told them she was from South

Africa, they did not appear surprised by her fair complexion.

Slowly she overcame her shyness and developed more confidence. She reserved a small amount of her weekly salary for new outfits that she picked up at a mill outlet.

When Bessy heard of Libka's job, she told Sara, "The Rabinovitzes are members of the temple, and Nina is active in the Sisterhood. You think they don't know Libka is my niece?"

"She didn't mention anything when she applied."

"You think Howie and Nina don't read the papers and the temple bulletin? They wanted to give her a break, my niece. Good Jewish people."

One afternoon Bessy wandered into the store, shuffling through the greeting cards, but the intention was to check on Libka's performance. Mr. Rabinovitz did not seem to know who she was. Libka treated her aunt formally; and Bessy, at a loss to find fault, never mentioned a word of this encounter to Sara.

During Sisterhood meetings the women would ask Bessy how the immigrant family was doing and she reported that her niece was working at the Rabinovitz stationery store.

"That will take a load off your hands," Mrs. Krinsky remarked. "After all, you have your own family to think of."

ooooo

After three months at the store, Libka asked permission to have Saturday afternoons off. Between school and working six days a week, she hardly saw her family and particularly missed Shneyer and Dina.

Not only did Mr. Rabinovitz grant her this right, he took the chance to increase her salary.

"My customers are very satisfied with you, Lorna, and I notice many people are returning since you joined us. Some even ask for you."

Libka started a pattern of taking Shneyer and Dina downtown on her afternoon off. Although she had opened a joint savings account with her mother, she set aside a small portion of her earnings for the children.

"How much money you got to spend?" Shneyer would always ask.

For his seventh birthday Libka planned a special treat. His hands laden with puzzles, trucks, soldiers and a top, he begged for some marbles. "Please. Just a hundred blue and green ones!"

"A hundred! Are you crazy? You'll get seven—one for every year."

"I want marbles too!" Dressed in her red coat and hat with white leggings, Dina clutched her little doll house and jumped up and down at the Woolworths toy rack.

"But, Dina, look what you already have."

"Just two marbles, Libki, and I'll put on my pants next time."

"Okay, but we still have more surprises."

The children's eyes were wide as they clung to Libka to find out what that would be.

"I'm not telling," she said. "Let's pay the lady first."

The next surprise was the soda fountain. Shneyer swivelled around in the high, red seat and Dina began to do the same.

"How come she's such a copy cat?" said Shneyer. "She doesn't even like marbles."

As Dina protested, Libka said, "Shh, you're both getting chocolate sundaes, so be quiet!"

"Shocolate shummies!" shouted Dina.

"She's a fool," said Shneyer. "She doesn't even know what a shundy is."

Dina was insulted. She looked at him, then at Libka, and burst into tears. "I do too know... I do too..."

She was wailing when the sundae was put before her, but her eyes popped out at the ice cream, cherries, nuts and chocolate sauce. She sucked in her nose, but with tears still dripping down her face, she dug into the dish.

"Wait a minute!" Libka stuck a napkin under her chin. "Don't dirty your coat."

Shneyer tried to appear casual as he ate the first sundae of his life, aware that Dina was peeking at his progress. Then she imitated him. When Shneyer spat out the cherry, Dina did the same.

"See that," he said, "she's a real copy cat."

Dina crinkled up her face. She caught Libka's eyes and her attempted wail petered out as she gobbled the sundae.

When they were finished, their faces smeared, Libka announced, "Now comes the biggest surprise."

The children hung on her as they strolled down Main Street and Dina began to pull faces.

"Doesn't she 'barrass you?" said Shneyer, cringing at Dina's flamboyance.

"She's having fun. Let her."

When Libka took out some money as they reached the movie theatre, Shneyer looked up at her in awe. "You still got more money?"

"Enough for the movies."

As they sauntered across the maroon-carpeted lobby, Libka whispered, "We're going to see *Snow White and the Seven Dwarves* and *Cinderella*."

The excitement of being in a dark theatre for the first time kept the children numb and silent. Libka sat between them, glancing from one to the other, their eyes glassy, lost in the magic of the screen. Dina would sometimes answer Snow White or one of the dwarves, believing she was part of their world, and Shneyer was so enwrapped in the fantasy that he didn't even notice.

At intermission Libka took them to the glass display in the lobby. Shneyer got a pack of hot popcorn, and Dina howled and said she wanted the same. Then Shneyer pointed to some red liquorice and was amazed when Libka agreed to buy it. "Well, it's your birthday."

Close to hysteria, Dina demanded the same.

"I'll get each of you a liquorice stick, but you have to share the popcorn."

"I don't want to share with her. She's a baby."

"Be good," said Libka. "You're seven years old."

Shoving her hand into the popcorn, Dina asked, "When will I be seven?"

"You're only three. It's four more years."

During the second movie, Dina began to make funny sounds, trying to amuse those around her, and Shneyer told Libka to keep her quiet. "Aren't you even 'barrassed for the people?" he whispered.

"She's only a baby," Libka whispered back.

Eventually Dina fell asleep; and when the movie ended, Libka had to awaken the rosy-cheeked Shneyer as well.

It was dark when they rode home in the bus, and Shneyer and Dina knelt in their seats, their eyes on the snow that was softly descending. It seemed like a magical world.

TWENTY-NINE

After Libka returned Melvin's ring, he shared his grief with his mother one night. "I can understand it," he tried to console himself, "she's only sixteen, though I originally thought she was older. Maybe I was putting too much pressure on her."

Libka had not told her mother about the occurrence at the Primrose Palace. "I guess he thinks I'm too young," was all she had managed to say. "I should have told him the truth from the beginning."

Melvin had called a few nights after that evening. He made no mention of the ring and asked if he could see her the following Saturday night.

She had chased her sister out of the bedroom and closed the door, and this time she spoke in the only way she could. "I don't think so, Melvin. I'm much too confused about my future to make any...promises..."

"You don't have to make any promises. Really! Like I told you, Lorna, there's no rush—really, no rush at all. And now, knowing that you're still younger, naturally I understand your point of view. So no pressure, I swear!"

She had thanked him over and over again, but said that somehow she did not feel right about it. "It's very hard for me to explain, but I feel I would be doing the wrong thing."

After much discomfort, they hung up, Melvin saying he would try her in a week or so to see if her mood might have changed. But he never called again.

"It is surprising," Libka heard her mother say to Beryl one night. "He like her and respect her, and New Year's Eve...like a princess she looked in the velvet outfit and the mink cape."

"Don't you think you're interfering too much?" said Beryl. "After all, it's her life."

Bessy, however, would not relent. Despite her estrangement toward Sara, she could not withhold her curiosity. "Still no word?"

"No," Sara answered flatly.

"Listen, to find out a girl is a few years younger is not such a crime. But if I was the young man and I found out that she had a bad reputation..."

"Worry about your own reputation," Sara snapped.

Mrs. Krinsky got wind of this development and became more active in the Sisterhood, using it as another opportunity to solicit information. "I was very sorry to hear that Melvin is no longer keeping company with the African girl," she told Mrs. Klein as Bessy looked on. They hoped for some disclosure from Mrs. Klein but she simply ignored the subject.

"What a pity! They seemed to be getting along so well," Mrs. Krinsky added. "I hope it was not a misunderstanding."

"That's not for me to answer," Mrs. Klein said.

"She knows more than she's letting on," Mrs. Krinsky whispered to Bessy when they were out of earshot, "and I'm sure she feels plenty of guilt for putting her nephew in touch with her."

Bessy resented the inference about her niece, despite her accusation to Sara. After all, how did it reflect on her?

"I think you've spent too much time meddling in this matter," she said curtly. "Are you hoping he'll call your daughter again?"

"Don't worry about my daughter," Mrs. Krinsky retorted. "She's doing very well, thank you."

"If I had such a daughter," said Bessy, "I'd be plenty worried." She turned away as Mrs. Krinsky eyed her, then gravitated to Mrs. Wolfson nearby.

"Have you found a reliable babysitter?" she inquired.

"Touch wood, we have. My husband is so thrilled that at last we have someone that the children adore."

It seemed that the rumour about her husband and Libka had not yet reached her.

"You've heard of course that Mrs. Klein's nephew has dropped your former babysitter."

"I'm not surprised. The mystery is why she ever introduced them."

"She must feel plenty of guilt. But Melvin is a bright boy and found out for himself."

To her daughter that night, Mrs. Krinsky remarked, "Just you wait, Melvin will come knocking at your door one of these days. Imagine getting involved with a slut like that. She should be driven out of this town."

THIRTY

Libka had almost forgotten about her application to Cambridge University when a response arrived advising that she had been accepted and offering a scholarship. It took her several days to absorb the news and share it with her mother. "I'm telling you privately," she said, "but I don't want you to breathe a word of it to anyone—not a word to that brother of yours and his wife."

"If that's what you want, I will respect your wishes, but is it something to be ashamed of?"

"They only bring bad luck and twist things."

When Libka informed her guidance counsellor at Little Falls High of this news, Miss Lee seemed proud but not surprised.

"Perhaps it's the higher level of the British educational system in Cape Town, but I felt you stood a good chance at Cambridge. Congratulations, Libka. Your mother must be very proud, and no doubt the scholarship being offered will be helpful."

Soon after this news arrived, Sara reviewed her certificates at the Citizens Savings Bank, which she had set up with various maturity dates. One sizable certificate would be maturing within three months and she would redeem the funds and earmark them for Libka's entry to Cambridge.

"It is wonderful that the university is offering you a scholarship," she said. "Of course it will still cost money, but for something like this I wouldn't hesitate."

Sara's enthusiasm for life improved. She took more interest in her appearance, knitting herself a pink cardigan with a fringed scarf and sewing a burgundy skirt with a slit in back. She discarded her torn hosiery and wore new silk stockings with the seam neatly aligned, and black pumps that propped up her height. She applied powder and lipstick, and a touch of blush to her cheeks. The piercings on her earlobes had sealed and she had them reopened at a jeweller, inserting the diamond earrings Mr. Garfinkel had once given her. She carried her head high and no longer climbed the fence into the woods to avoid the neighbours. She sometimes attended Saturday services at Temple Emmanuel and mingled with the congregation. When asked how the family was faring, she replied, "My children are all doing very well."

In this spirit of optimism, with Libka's consent, she sent a letter off to Abe Garfinkel informing him of Libka's acceptance at Cambridge. Though Garfinkel no longer wrote regularly, Sara now had the confidence to hint that perhaps they would meet again. *With Andrew in England and now Libka, it gives more reason to believe that one day we will see each other again.* When Sara reread these words the day after writing them, she thought perhaps she was being too assertive, but decided to mail the letter.

Life took on greater meaning and even the hard work at the laundromat seemed to have more purpose. It enabled her to cover the daily expenses of the household, and she was relieved not to reach into the savings for anything other than unusual events. There were few luxuries, but no one went hungry and nor did the family have to depend on anyone for charity.

She believed that when it came to education, money was an investment, and she knew that Yosef would have shared this conviction. Libka deserved this support since she had excelled in her studies despite the adjustment to a new country.

In planning to send Libka to London, Sara resolved that she would not expose her to any humiliation. She was extremely touchy and sensitive, and since Yosef's death it was sometimes impossible to talk to her. Sara was aware that Libka had suffered most from the relocation to Little Falls. It was no better a place for her than Cape Town had been. Meyer and Bessy only made things worse, condemning her for not being outgoing and sociable.

There was something else that preyed on Sara's mind, though she had never verbalized it to anyone. Was there any truth to Bessy's disclosure that Libka was seen in a parked car in the woods with Mr. Wolfson?

In London she would be able to make a new beginning. Garfinkel's son Andrew would be devoted to her. They had been so close in their childhood when the families would summer together in Muizenberg. And she would reunite with Anya.

ooooo

You are the first person with whom I'm sharing this news other than my mother and my guidance counsellor at school, Libka wrote Anya when the reality settled in. *I've been accepted at Cambridge and they're offering me a scholarship. So it appears that we will see each other again after all! The truth is, Anya, when we parted in Southampton I did not think we would ever meet again.*

She was careful not to reveal her feelings about Sayyed. She could not disclose to Anya that her real yearning to go to London was to reunite with him.

Libka sent the letter off by registered air mail and saved the receipt from the postal clerk.

In the weeks that followed, every time she came home from work she eagerly checked the mail. She had even imagined that upon receiving this news, Anya might send a telegram. But as time passed she grew anxious. She would soon have to submit her acceptance to the university, but she felt she had to hear from Anya before doing so. In a way, it would confirm that this dream was a reality.

After a while Libka began to wonder if her letter had reached her friend. She inquired at the post office, showing the receipt, but the clerk informed her that there was no indication that the letter had not reached its destination.

Though Libka had a telephone number for Anya's sister at her university office, it seemed too radical to phone. She thought of sending a telegram, but held back.

She had almost given up when she came home one day and Beryl proffered a blue envelope. "From England!" As he presented it to Libka ceremoniously, he sang:

God save our gracious King,
Long live our noble King,
God save the King:
Send him victorious,
Happy and glorious,
Long to reign over us:
God save the King.

"Oh, stop!" Libka noticed the letter was from Anya. She snatched it from her brother's hands and ran upstairs.

Dear Libka,

You must excuse the long delay in answering your exciting letter, but many things have happened in my life. I guess mostly the miracle: I am in love. You wouldn't know me anymore. I am not the same angry girl you once knew. And it's not a British lad who has stolen my heart. You will never believe who brought about this change in me.

Love! You may wonder what I know about that. All I knew at home was hatred and misery. Anyway, those days are over.

Libka, I assure you when you come to England we won't get into any fights, like the one that got you expelled from Promenade Junior High. How could you ever forgive me? And yet we became the closest friends. You're still my best friend.

Don't misunderstand me. It's not as though I've lost my passion. I'm as fiery as ever but it's directed to a worthy cause. These days I'm fighting for racial equality. Is it any wonder, coming from South Africa? I always hated the way the whites acted as though they were kings, all at the expense of the Bantus and coloureds. And the Malays.

Remember when we went to see Maputo in prison and you were so shattered at the sight of him that you forgot to give him the biltong you had stolen from your pantry and the feather pillow from Lithuania?

Anyway, now from England there can be hope, and when you come here we can join together to fight for our beliefs.

Are you dying to know who brought about this transformation in me? I enclose a photo. I think you will recognize the guilty parties. Yes, the object of my love is a man you once met on an isolated beach in Cape Town. We can never thank you enough for bringing us together. We're sharing a small flat. My sister approves. She agrees that when two people are as madly in love as Sayyed and I, we should be together. Modest as our quarters are, there will always be room for you, Libka, and Sayyed and I will do everything we can to help you get settled.

Libka studied the picture of Anya and Sayyed. As the fortune-teller had prophesized: a man of yellow skin and a girl with green eyes. As they held each other close, they were as radiant as the stars Libka had seen in films. Anya's eyes, which had always held defiance, were now filled with tenderness, and her raven hair flowed to her waist. Was it any mystery that Sayyed had been smitten by her?

THIRTY-ONE

Sara was closing the laundromat earlier on Wednesdays because Golda could only relieve her a few afternoons a week due to her music lessons. "It is more important that Golda develop her talent in music than drag dirty laundry after school, so we will take in a few dollars less. We will manage." Golda was also babysitting and saving every penny in the hope of someday buying a piano.

On this Wednesday, Sara decided to prepare a festive meal—soup with kreplach, roast chicken and potatoes and cabbage rolls. Early that morning, before going to the laundromat, she had made bagels and a honey cake.

In an attempt to lighten Libka's grim moods, she was serving better meals and not skimping on meat. She was worried about her daughter's silence but was careful not to question her. Perhaps the impending move to England was overwhelming to her.

"We will eat in the dining room today," Sara announced.

"What's the occasion?"

"Never mind, Libkala." Sara eyed her mysteriously.

Libka's gloom was so heavy that it permeated the house, even affecting the younger children. Shneyer would sometimes tickle Libka's toes to try to cheer her up. He knew what sadness was, remembering when his father disappeared from his life and the children danced in front of his old house, chanting:

Sayer can't play! Sayer can't play!
Not today! Not today!

His daddy is dead dead dead!
So Sayer must stay in bed bed bed!

Beryl too was more considerate toward Libka, though he couldn't fathom why she seemed gloomy when so much adventure awaited her. "Hey," he'd say, "do you want to go in the bathroom first? I may be quite a while." This gentle treatment sometimes made Libka cry and she would remain locked in the bathroom, dabbing at her red eyes, ashamed to show her emotions.

Libka had not been able to tell her mother of Anya's letter and nor had she submitted her acceptance to Cambridge.

How could she explain her feelings? She hardly knew the Malay boy. Yet her sense of betrayal did not diminish. If Anya could do this to her, she would never want to see her again.

One night when she came home from work, Beryl greeted her with a telegram. He hoped this would raise her spirits. "Guess from who?"

Libka grabbed it and saw it was from Anya.

Beryl watched her excitedly, hoping it would produce a smile. "I happened to be home when it was delivered. Imagine, a telegram! I guess Anya can't wait for you to be in England."

Sara clasped her hands. "Remember, Libkala, how you and Anya cried at the docks in Southampton? Who would dream that one day you would be together again?"

Libka ran upstairs, closing her bedroom door. *CONCERND BY LONG SILENCE. CAN'T WAIT FOR YOU TO BE HERE. LOVE, ANYA.*

ooooo

Buoyed by Libka's acceptance at Cambridge, Sara did not mind the long hours at the laundromat, though she had little help. Golda had to fetch Shneyer from his primary school in addition to her music lessons in the afternoon. Dina's care was a problem. Sara occasionally managed to leave her with a neighbour, but often the child tagged along with her, playing with her wetting doll on the cement floor.

Sara realized it had been over two months since she sent off the letter to Abe Garfinkel, informing him of Libka's acceptance at Cambridge. She was in the habit of keeping a copy of the letters she sent him, alongside his letters to her, and now she reached for the wooden chest beneath her bed and opened it. As she reread her letter, she was embarrassed at her statement, *With Andrew in England and now Libka, it gives us more reason to believe that one day we can meet again.* She had never expressed herself so openly to him, yet would it not be more reason for him to respond?

Late one day when Sara returned from the laundromat, Beryl announced that there was a letter from South Africa.

"Who is it from?" Sara asked, secretly hoping that Abe Garfinkel had at last responded.

"Nothing important," said Beryl, "only Mrs. Peker."

ooooo

After the children had eaten and Dina was asleep in her cot, Sara climbed into bed. Her knees were stiff and aching, and she switched on the heating pad, then opened the letter from Riva Peker. In English that seemed to grow worse with every letter, she boasted about her daughters. Sally was already married to the rich boy whose father owned a scrap metal business and she was expecting a baby. They had bought a house in Sea Point. Her other three daughters were dating rich young men from Sea Point and The Gardens. Servants were her main problem. She had to discharge one girl because she showed no respect and she discovered another one was stealing. *You have to watch these* shvartzes *like hawks!*

Sara flipped the sheet over and her eyes fell on the name Garfinkel. *My Sally told me that at a fancy restaurant in Sea Point one night she saw Abe Garfinkel with a lady—a beautiful blond lady wearing a big diamond on her wedding finger. Well, Garfinkel can afford it.*

In her jumbled script she went on to say that a widower like Garfinkel doesn't remain alone forever. *Listen, he was a catch—one in a million. You had your chance to have a luxurious life in his Camps*

Bay mansion with a staff of servants. How many servants do you have now? I hope your life in America is so good.

Sara folded the letter, turned off the lamp and went to sleep.

Though she tried to dispel Riva Peker's words, they lingered in her mind. Could Abe Garfinkel ever have cared for her if she had been replaced so soon?

When Sara least expected it, Libka entered her room one night, appearing to be in a lighter mood. "How come you haven't asked about Anya?"

She sat down on Sara's bed, stretching out her bare feet. "There's nothing worse than being betrayed by your best friend."

Sara lifted her eyes from the book she was reading. "You had an argument with Anya?"

"I might as well show you!" Libka dashed to her room and returned with Anya's letter. After she had read it to her mother, Sara asked, "And this is why you didn't write to her again?"

"And why I'm not going to London!"

Sara closed her book and stared into space. She was mystified by Libka's decision.

"Well, do you think it's right?" Libka insisted. "How would you feel if Mr. Garfinkel started going out with another woman?"

Did Libka sense something? Did she know something?

"I will tell you, Libkala," her mother finally said, "it looks like Mr. Garfinkel is engaged to somebody else."

How could this be? He had been in love with her mother, helping with the problems in the factory, remaining at her side during the tragic news from Europe, even obtaining the visas for America, though it broke his heart. Libka knew that in parting they hoped that one day they might be together again.

After hearing that Mr. Garfinkel had another woman, Libka was gentler with her mother. When Beryl made demands on Sara, Libka would defend her. "Mommy works hard enough in the laundromat all day. Can't you do something for yourself?"

She no longer stayed after hours at the stationery store. She and Golda alternated picking up the younger children. A neighbour, whose boy went to the same primary school as Shneyer, started taking him to her place, and Dina was left with another neighbour. Libka tried to arrive home with the children before Sara stumbled in. They were hungry and tired. She would give them milk and cookies. She peeled potatoes, carrots and onions, but was sparing with the meat. Then she would heat a pot of water so that her mother could have tea when she came home.

Libka knew Sara was heartbroken that she had declined the scholarship at Cambridge and many times she questioned her own decision. She was as perplexed about her emotions as her mother was.

She found herself brooding over her mother's position and felt guilty for being a burden. If anyone had a right to feel betrayed, it was Sara. Mr. Garfinkel had become a part of their lives and now he was with another woman.

THIRTY-TWO

As the time for graduation approached, the shop windows displayed chiffon gowns in white and pastels, the mannequins like brides. Girls strolled down after school to marvel over the displays, and mothers often accompanied them into the shops. There was talk of boys to invite to the prom.

One Saturday afternoon Bessy arrived with a large plastic bag. Sara was at the laundromat and Libka had taken Shneyer and Dina downtown for their weekly treat. Beryl had gone off in a convertible with his friends. Only Golda was home, studying and reviewing her music books.

"Hello, Gail. I'm just dropping this off. Libka not home?"

"No," said Golda, but did not offer any details.

"When she gets home, give her this." She pushed the bag into Golda's hands.

Golda was too discreet to look inside but left the bag on Libka's bed.

"Aunt Bessy brought you something," she informed her sister when she came home.

Libka peeked inside the bag and pulled out a long dark dress that looked like a petticoat. It brought back memories of the Hadassah sack that had landed on their porch soon after their arrival in America.

When Sara came home, Libka led her upstairs and showed her the garment. "Golda said Bessy left it for me. What's it for?"

Sara lifted the limp piece of clothing. "I don't think it is suitable for your high school graduation."

The previous night Bessy had informed Sara that she was dropping off a gown for Libka's graduation. "I hope it will fit. The length should be all right."

Twenty years earlier Bessy had worn this garment to a relative's wedding in the Bronx and it had remained in plastic ever since. "Only once I wore it. It's like new."

"I'm not wearing this," Libka told her mother.

"Don't worry, my child, we will buy you a gown like all the other girls."

"I can use my own money," offered Libka.

"I can still afford to buy you a graduation gown. May you wear in good health."

The following Saturday afternoon Beryl stayed in the laundromat for a few hours while Sara took Libka to the store where she had bought the trousseau for dates with Melvin. The saleslady seemed to recognize them.

"Oh, you're the people from Africa. How are you adjusting to America?" she asked. "Quite a difference, huh? What wonderful relatives you have. They deserve the recognition by Temple Emmanuel."

Would she ever hear the end of it! Libka thought. And here she had to listen to this when she felt like a bloated goose in the chiffon gown with the crinoline. But her mother looked so pleased that she agreed to take it.

"It needs a few inches off the bottom," the saleslady said. "Would you like us to alter it?"

Sara responded swiftly. "No, thank you. I can handle."

Though she didn't expect Libka to grow any taller, Golda would be graduating in a few years and she would need the additional length. Meanwhile, Sara would make a temporary hem for Libka's graduation.

"The gown would also be suitable for the prom," Sara said, "but of course you won't invite Melvin."

"Have you noticed that I don't get the cramps anymore?"

"I was telling Golda the other night. You don't buy the Pepto Bismol."

"Maybe now you know why I used to get those cramps."

"Whatever it was," said Sara, "let us be grateful that it is gone."

Libka surprised everyone by inviting Matt to the prom. He was out of the hospital and had called her. "I want to tell you, Lorna, your visit gave me a lift and I had a great time with you on Christmas night."

He arrived in his father's Mercedes, wearing a tuxedo; and as she came down the porch steps he handed her a corsage. When they entered the hall, all eyes turned to them. They looked like a happy bride and groom.

THIRTY-THREE

Every morning Sara went off to the laundromat when it was still dark, often dragging a half-sleeping Dina. And at the end of a long day she would sometimes have to wait over half an hour for the bus downtown, where she would transfer for the one cruising near her home. Her arms were always laden with bags of laundry and groceries that she would buy downtown, and she was out of breath when she finally got home.

"Listen, Mom," Beryl said, "we have to get a car. Most families here have two cars and we drag around like gypsies."

"Rich man," said Sara, "who will pay the expenses?"

"I'll take care of it, Mom, don't worry!"

With savings from working in his uncle's mill, Beryl bought a used Pontiac from a dealer.

"Instead of your dragging around with two buses and waiting for hours, I'll deposit you right at your doorstep."

"You want to make a queen of me?" Sara said, but felt proud of her son.

Beryl was inspired by Libka, who seemed to have calmed down. She wasn't so emotional and critical. She was also of more help. She made the beds, vacuumed, mopped the floors in the kitchen and bathroom, and often prepared supper or laid the table. After a meal, she would sometimes nudge her mother away from the sink. "Go upstairs and rest, Mom. I'll do the dishes."

"There are signs that Libka is pulling herself together too," Beryl remarked in Libka's presence. "I don't know what brought about the change but I'm not complaining."

"Thank you," said Libka, "but I don't need your compliments."

Beryl chuckled and ruffled Libka's hair before galloping upstairs to get ready for the evening.

Beryl was aware of Libka's acceptance at the university in England, but it didn't seem Libka was going after all. When he asked her, she replied, "What makes you think I'm moving? Don't be in such a hurry to get rid of me."

Though there was a time when he would have liked to see her leave the house, she was far more tolerable these days, and he knew that Shneyer and Dina were close to her. She was patient with them and they looked forward to Saturdays when she took them downtown for treats. He had to admit that now he would miss Libka if she left.

ooooo

That July life seemed promising. Libka and Beryl were both working. The stationery store was satisfied with Libka, and Mr. Rabinovitz had asked about her future plans. "I don't have any plans right now," she answered, to which he responded, "Can we offer you a full-time position? We're taking in a line of Underwood typewriters, so we expect a more brisk business."

Beryl had given up his job at his uncle's mill and was working at the yacht club. Each morning he dressed in sailor attire and looked like a prince when he set out. He was exuberant and cheerful, whistling and dancing the *kazatska* to amuse his mother. "Stop already, Beryl," she would joke. Sometimes he would entwine her in his arms and waltz her around the kitchen as she protested and laughed.

Beryl would be studying textile design at Bryant Technical Institute in the fall.

"Now that we have a car, Mom," he said, "I could likely even work after school and on weekends, so it will more than pay off. Uncle Meyer was so opposed to my having an education, but you were right to be insistent. And Dad would have felt the same way."

"Of course," Sara said, masking her tears.

The younger children were doing well too. Golda was studying music and babysitting for the Goldsteins, who treated her kindly. They had three small children, and Shneyer and Dina could always be left at their house, which was on the same street. Often they would invite Golda over a little earlier so she could have supper with their children. On such occasions Mrs. Goldstein served pizza, chocolate chip cookies and ice cream. She would ask Golda what flavour she liked, and give her the choice of chocolate, vanilla or strawberry.

"What good children they are," Golda told Sara. "They go to bed without any trouble, and the older boy even offers me ice cream and cookies when I study. Quite a difference from what Libka had to put up with at that other family."

"I admire your mother," Mrs. Goldstein told Golda. "She's done an admirable job with you children, and all on her own." Although their house was only five doors away, Mr. Goldstein always walked Golda home at the end of an evening and frequently wedged an extra quarter or two into her hand. "Buy something special for your little brother and sister."

Libka had abandoned the thought of moving to London and her earnings made many things possible. She bought a few new lamps for the living room and carpeting for the stairway to the bedrooms, which Beryl installed. And on Sara's forty-fifth birthday she and Beryl arrived in his Pontiac and carried in a mahogany console that not only had television but radio as well.

Sara, flushed with amazement, pleaded that they return it. "I don't need such luxuries—to have a movie theatre in my home." But Libka would be thrilled to catch her perched on the couch, eyes glowing as she watched a movie when the children had gone to sleep.

Earlier that summer Beryl had given Sara driving lessons. Though the children were amused when she first got into the driver's seat, which Beryl adjusted to make her legs reach the pedals, she had shown surprising ability. They would practice driving up and down the dead-end street, and Beryl would often have to restrain her. "Slow down, Mom. What's your hurry?"

Sara would laugh breathlessly. "I never dreamed that one day I would drive a car in America."

Beryl would take her to remote areas where they would practice parking. The car would sometimes jolt as she'd cry "Oy!" Often the children would catch her chuckling at the sink as she washed the dishes and they knew what she was thinking.

"Now you'll have a few professional lessons," Beryl said one day, "and then you're on your own."

She passed the driving test on the first attempt. Thereafter, Beryl announced, "I've joined a carpool of guys who work at the yacht club. They all have cars, so we'll be taking turns. The car is all yours, Mom."

Early one morning Beryl appeared in the kitchen as Sara was making bagels. "Drop everything! You're driving to the laundromat."

After Sara had driven alone on several occasions, she developed more confidence. It seemed like a miracle to be able to put the huge bag of laundry in the trunk and then hop into the car and set off down the street. In the evening she would stop off at the general store and buy a gallon of milk. As she'd turn onto her street, she'd be pleased to see the neighbours watching as she revved the engine, and she'd wave regally.

Shneyer and Dina were in a summer program where they often went on camping expeditions, and it was Golda's duty to tend to them. She would prepare their breakfast, help them dress, and deliver them and pick them up. The meeting grounds were ten minutes from the house and they would stroll over.

That summer the machines in the laundromat operated smoothly; and if there was a problem Beryl would repair them at night. "They work better than new," Sara would remark, proud of her handsome son. "Like your father. You have magic hands."

Libka also obtained a driver's licence that summer; and one Saturday she jumped into the car and kept driving on the highway. After an hour she saw signs to Boston and decided to head in that direction. Though slightly overwhelmed when she approached the traffic of the city, she parked on a side street and spent the day roaming through the commons and gardens. She went into Filene's Basement and rummaged through the racks. Now that she had an account at the Citizens Savings Bank in Little Falls, she felt independent. Sara no longer made her clothes, and Libka would allot a small portion of her earnings for a new item.

Though Libka was more peaceful at home and had no regrets about her decision to remain, she felt that one day she would leave Little Falls. Beryl could drive her to Providence and she would take a milk train to New York. She had passed through the great city when the ship from Southampton landed in the Port of New York, and she dreamed of one day exploring it on her own.

Several months passed before she was able to respond to Anya's letter and telegram. *There are so many changes in my life right now,* she wrote, *that I think it's best I delay my move at this time.* She did not feel ready to reveal the pain it had caused her and nor was she able to express happiness that she and Sayyed were together. She knew that was how she should feel, and maybe a day would come when they could even laugh about it.

She had become closer to her mother and was now able to share personal things.

"I have to make a confession," she said one night. "Melvin and I didn't break up because I was only sixteen."

"I never believed that, but I didn't want to question you."

"On New Year's Eve he gave me a ring, but I couldn't accept it."

Sara did not seem disappointed. "It was wrong for everybody to push you when you didn't like him. I realize a person can't choose for somebody else."

"I thought you'd be annoyed."

"No, Libkala. When I was a girl in Lithuania, I had a similar experience. You know my mother was also a struggling widow and I didn't have a dowry, but there was a man who wanted to marry me and take me to Palestine. I was already twenty-six and my mother was so happy. But I couldn't take the step."

"So what happened?"

"Daddy came to our town to manage the Jewish People's Bank

and I was working there. He was engaged to a girl from another town, but she had an older sister that the matchmakers couldn't find a husband for, so he waited and waited. He was already close to thirty when we got married and left for South Africa."

"You and Daddy really loved each other, didn't you?"

"Right from the beginning."

Libka hesitated before she said, "But I think you also liked Mr. Garfinkel."

"I never dreamed it was possible after Yosef."

THIRTY-FOUR

Beryl would sometimes allow Libka to borrow his Pontiac and she'd head for the hurricane-ravaged beach she loved. The isolated ocean rekindled memories of Three Anchor Bay. She would climb the rocks and dive into the waters, coasting like a seal.

One Sunday when she and Shneyer were exploring this stretch of ocean, they came upon a trailer that seemed abandoned. They were fascinated by this structure with portholes through which one could peek. An old fisherman walked by and saw them hovering around the trailer. "You want to live there, children?"

"Does somebody live here?" Libka inquired.

"No, dearie. An old seaman used to make his home here..oh, maybe ten, fifteen years ago."

Shneyer too was intrigued by the trailer, climbing near the opening, and Libka asked the fisherman if they could look inside.

The man released the door and Libka and Shneyer climbed in. There were rooms like in a house, a kitchen with a fridge and gas burner, and a toilet and sink.

"Do you think anything works?" she asked the man.

He tested the appliances.

"Everything works. Just close it up before you leave." He gathered his fishing gear.

"If I want to live here, what do I do?" Libka asked.

"See the little stand up the hill?" The man pointed. "There's a woman who sells hot dogs and ice cream. She can tell you."

Libka and Shneyer explored the trailer and decided to find the woman.

"There's a trailer on the beach," Libka said as the woman smothered ketchup and relish on a hot dog.

"Yes, I know, honey. What about it?"

"Can I rent it?"

She looked at Libka and Shneyer and laughed. "You kids don't have a home or something?"

"My mother would come too. Can we stay there for a weekend?"

"You have my blessing, sweetie."

"We can pay you."

"Just leave it tidy when you take off. That's all I ask. It used to belong to my old man, but he's long since passed on."

∞∞∞∞∞

Libka was determined to bring the family to the trailer for a weekend and arranged to take a full day off on a Saturday. To make up for that, she worked on Saturday afternoons twice in a row, eliminating the treats with Shneyer and Dina. On the second Saturday afternoon, a stout woman ambled into the store leaning on a walker. She made her way over to the section on cards for special occasions. She seemed familiar yet Libka could not place her. She waited a moment then went over and asked if she could help. The woman turned abruptly and Libka was startled by the hostility in the eyes that swept over her from head to toe.

"Oh, I suppose you don't know me, but I'm a close friend of your aunt. My name is Mrs. Krinsky. I'm looking for something special. Do you have a section on engagements?"

Libka pointed to the cards for engagements and weddings.

"It's for my daughter's engagement. She's a busy girl and doesn't have time to look around."

"Well, congratulations," Libka faltered.

"A fine young man has fallen for her. You may know of him— Melvin Kaplan."

Libka wondered whether Mrs. Krinsky's story was true. She knew that Melvin was eager to settle down and suspected Mrs. Krinsky's daughter was too. She recalled Aunt Bessy saying they had once dated.

"I read that article in the *Little Falls Chronicle* about your family. I'm sure it isn't easy being newcomers in America. Does your mother still run that laundromat in the Portuguese section?"

Libka nodded.

"Poor thing. I used to see her dragging the heavy bags at night. If I still drove my Lincoln, I would have given her a ride, but I'm not young anymore."

A customer entered and Libka tried to escape, but Mrs. Krinsky restrained her.

"Is this all you have?" She shuffled through the cards. "Frankly, I don't see anything suitable. I thought I'd pop in, but my daughter will drive me to Boston where they'll surely have a decent selection."

"That's fine."

"Just one word and it shows—your African accent. I understand you used to babysit for the Wolfsons. A lovely family. And such well-behaved children, as you would expect of parents like that."

Much as Libka loved her family, she realized she would have to build a life elsewhere.

THIRTY-FIVE

When Sara closed the laundromat at one o'clock on Wednesdays, she would load the bags of fresh laundry into the car and drive to the supermarket for shopping. She would fill the cart with potatoes, onions, carrots and often a chuck roast or turkey, which could provide at least two meals for the family with meat left over for sandwiches.

On this particular Wednesday she had an omen that she would hear from Abe Garfinkel. Though she had tried to dismiss him from her mind since reading Riva Peker's letter, she had dreamed of him the previous night. They were sitting on the veranda of his Camps Bay villa, the birds trilling. The palms swayed and the scent of the tropical flowers and honeysuckles filled the air. They could hear the pounding of the ocean down below. Garfinkel reached for her hand. "Sara, you have brought me happiness." His words were so real that when she awoke she was startled to find herself in the bedroom in Little Falls, Dina asleep in the cot.

Although Sara usually slipped into the house through the rear door, dragging in the bundles, this time she went up the front steps, eager to check the mail. It was as though Garfinkel had read her thoughts, for on the porch lay a letter from him.

ooooo

Sara eyed the letter in disbelief. It had been so long since she had written him about Libka's acceptance at Cambridge that she had given up hope of a response. She hurried upstairs and opened the envelope. Sitting on her bed, she read the Hebrew words:

My beloved Sara, if you have given up on me, I do not blame you. It may seem unforgivable that I did not respond to your letter in which you advised me of Libka's acceptance at Cambridge. It arrived at a time of great turmoil in my life. Our beloved Eliza, who had been in our household for almost thirty years, passed away just days before your letter arrived. Of course it was not unexpected. She had been ailing for many years. But to lose her was like losing a family member since she was so close with Hena and the children, whom she raised. It consoled me, however, that she died peacefully. One morning she did not appear in the kitchen—and later when I went to check in her room she was lying in bed. I called her name and she did not answer, and then I realized that she had passed away. Though she was not able to do much for many years, her presence was reassuring to me.

Now all this seems like a poor excuse for my silence. You can imagine how I felt at your words that someday we might meet in London. I read those words many times and they sustained me because when we parted, you may remember I had expressed such a hope.

I can now write you, my dear Sara, that I believe this will be possible. When Hena died, I did not imagine that I could love another, but with you I discovered that there was still room in my heart. I have been very lonely without you. I tried to fill the emptiness but to no avail. I had felt that I should remain in Cape Town because of Shoshana and Simon, who are building families here, but they have their own lives. I am selling my place in Camps Bay and looking into immigration to England. My company is running well and in time I may liquidate it.

By now I imagine that Libka is preparing to relocate to London. I have informed Andrew of this and he will help her get settled and do whatever he can to make her welcome. He

remembers Libka well and he is not surprised she was accepted
at Cambridge. You'll recall that as youngsters they played to-
gether so harmoniously during our summers in Muizenberg.

Please find it in your heart to forgive my long silence, my
dear Sara, and I shall be watching the mail daily for word
from you. I will now say what I have felt for a long time: I
love you, Sara.

She had gone upstairs around eleven after the children were asleep, but her mind was so full of thoughts that she tiptoed down again. She was drinking tea in the kitchen when Beryl returned from a night around town. It was past midnight. Usually he dashed up to his room without acknowledging her, so Sara was surprised when he leaned against the stove and asked, "So you think it's good we came to America, Mom?"

"I think you are satisfied, Beryl."

"Aren't you, Mom, especially now that you're driving like a Yankee?"

Sara looked at her son with pride. Golden from the sun and working on boats, he looked striking in his white attire, joy radiating in his face.

"As long as my children are happy, I am too."

Beryl reached in the fridge for a coke. "Libka and I are turning out all right, after all, don't you think, Mom? We weren't off to a very good start, but things are improving. And I think you're pleased that I'll be continuing my studies."

"Of course. I would not dream otherwise."

"And Libka seems to have pulled herself together."

"Well, she is maturing."

"Like the other morning I stayed in the bathroom too long, but she didn't bang on the door. Just tapped and said, 'Did you fall asleep?'" Beryl chuckled. "It seems some people have more than one bathroom in their house. Well, take our uncle and aunt, they're only a family of four and they have a bathroom upstairs and another one downstairs."

"Things are changing."

"And I can't wait for the day when we'll have a phone to ourselves. Every time I pick it up there's someone on the line."

"Most people have party lines."

"But you never know who's listening to your conversation."

Beryl lingered around the stove.

"How come you're up so late, Mom? Is the arthritis bothering you again?"

"No. I will go soon to bed."

Sara's mind was filled with the words from Abe Garfinkel. She had abandoned all hope of ever hearing from him after receiving Riva Peker's letter. She had repressed the tenderness she held for him. Never in their time together in Cape Town had he verbalized his feelings so directly, never had he said "I love you."

It was as if Beryl sensed something. Though he had enjoyed the outings on Mr. Garfinkel's yacht and double-dating with Simon and his girlfriend, he had assumed his mother had put the relationship into the past.

"By the way, Mom," he now asked, "do you ever hear from Mr. Garfinkel?"

Sara was not sure how to reply to Beryl's question, just as she was uncertain how she would respond to Garfinkel's letter.

"As you know, Mr. Garfinkel is still in Cape Town."

"How do you think Simon is doing in Dad's engineering factory?"

"I believe he's doing well. He graduated engineering from Cape Town University, and you remember he apprenticed with Daddy during the summers."

Beryl lingered, but Sara said, "Go to sleep already, Beryl. I will also go soon."

But she remained in the kitchen for many hours. She allowed herself to recapture the feelings she had for Abe Garfinkel. It was over two years since they had been together. She had never believed anyone other than Yosef could stir her so deeply. From afar the feelings seemed magnified, poetic and mysterious.

She thought of sending Garfinkel a telegram, expressing her love, but that seemed reckless. After all, she was a woman of forty-five, a widow with five children. It might be something one could read in books, but it could not happen in her life.

The first signs of morning were creeping into the house when she tiptoed upstairs and peeked into the bedrooms where her children slept. In her room, Dina lay cuddled in her cot with her new doll. Sara smiled at the child's sweet expression, then slipped into bed.

THIRTY-SIX

Bessy heard the thud of the newspaper on her terrace and pattered to the screen door. Each morning she eagerly awaited delivery of the *Little Falls Chronicle*. Next to the temple bulletin, it provided her with news of the town. The first items she generally checked were the obituaries because she had been volunteering at the Jewish Home for the Aged and knew many of the residents. She also avidly checked engagements and weddings, births and Bar Mitzvahs. There was always something happening in the town and it was important for her to keep abreast. When meeting with the other volunteers at the temple, she liked to be the first to announce new developments.

On this morning what captured her eye was an item near the front of the paper: *Local Resident Accused Of Sexual Misconduct.* The name Joel Wolfson rose out of the article.

> *A respected long-time resident of this community, Joel Wolfson, has been accused of sexual misconduct with a minor who was serving in his household as babysitter. The girl cannot be identified, but sources say she comes from the Flint district and was attending junior high school. Mr. Wolfson, who serves on the board of Temple Emmanuel, has denied the allegation. He is the father of three children, and will be arraigned in district court next Thursday.*

It was not yet eight o'clock but Bessy fled to the phone. She shuffled through her address book and dialled Sharon Krinsky's number. They had not been on congenial terms for some time, but she overlooked that.

Mrs. Krinsky answered on the first ring. She did not sleep well at night and spent most of her time chatting on the phone or looking out of her window. Her arthritic legs made it difficult for her to navigate the steps of her tenement.

"It's me—Bessy Marcus. Have you seen this morning's paper?"

Mrs. Krinsky complained that deliveries were not on schedule, so Bessy took pleasure in reading the article to her. Though she felt distant toward Sara and Libka, they were relatives after all, and she knew Sharon Krinsky had spread gossip about Libka that must have ended her relationship with Melvin Kaplan.

Mrs. Krinsky was unusually silent after hearing the article. Normally she would have thrived on such news, but she sensed Bessy's virtuous tone and felt the woman was getting back at her. Also, it was not good news. This public disclosure about Mr. Wolfson would discredit her efforts to stain Libka's reputation.

"Plenty of innocent people get falsely accused," she said. "I have never seen anything but graciousness in Mr. Wolfson. I'll have to check into that."

When her paper appeared at the door, she clipped out the article, dating it, and went to wake Fanny. "Have you ever read anything so preposterous?"

Bessy was uncertain whether to phone Sara. They had not been in touch for a number of weeks. Despite what she felt about Sharon Krinsky, she enjoyed needling her sister-in-law. By disclosing this information about Mr. Wolfson, all she had implied about Libka would not be credible.

Though Sara rarely read the *Little Falls Chronicle* and kept thinking of cancelling delivery, it happened that Beryl had noticed the article and brought it into the kitchen.

"How do you like that?" he said, and read, "'Local resident accused of sexual misconduct'—guess who? None other than Joel

Wolfson. Isn't that the family Libka was babysitting for?"

When Libka came home from work that night, Sara showed her the article.

"Libkala, you never complained about Mr. Wolfson. Did he act right with you?"

Sara thought of Bessy's incriminating statement about Libka in the parking lot with him. Though it troubled her deeply, she was never able to raise the issue.

Libka scanned the article. "He's a monster. The whole family is rotten. And I can thank Aunt Bessy for getting me that job."

"The truth comes out, my child," Sara consoled her. "It sometimes takes a while but the truth comes out."

THIRTY-SEVEN

Sara felt her family was adjusting to the new land. A year earlier she would not have envisioned how her two eldest, Beryl and Libka, could transform in such a responsible way. Beryl had become concerned about the family. He often gave up his car even on weekends so Sara could shop and drive the younger children to various places. He thrived on his work at the yacht club where he was always surrounded by friends and admirers.

Even more heartening to Sara were the changes in Libka. She was no longer as moody and critical, and one day she remarked, "Mama, I'm lucky to have such a nice family, so why should I run off to England? It was different for Anya, living in terror with that father."

"My child, you should do what you feel is best, but not every girl can get a scholarship to Cambridge University."

"Do you feel terrible that I turned it down?"

Sara shrugged. "It is not up to me. As Beryl say, it is your life, but of course I was very proud that they made you this offer."

"Do you think it was a mistake for us to come to America?"

"The important thing is for my children to make a good adjustment."

Libka took some apple juice from the fridge and sat down at the table opposite her mother.

"Do you know, Mom, that I kept all the letters you wrote me when I was at boarding school?"

Sara looked embarrassed. "You kept such documents?"

Libka ran upstairs and came down with a metal box. She leafed through the material and handed Sara a letter.

My darling daughter Libkala,
Everything at home is fine, but I think there will be good changes for all of us. South Africa has not been so good for us, especially for you, and my brother Meyer keep writing that we should consider America. Maybe it would be better. What do you think?
It is hard for me to write too much in English and it would be better if we can talk, but in the meantime please don't worry about anything. Better things will happen for our family.
Your loving mother, brothers and sisters

"Uncle Meyer seemed like such a nice man," Libka said. "Why did he change like that?"

"I remember when I went to our *landsleit,* the Shevahs, after I got Meyer's letter. Rochel warned me. 'Go maybe just for a few months with the small children and see how it is. It is many years since you saw your brother, and who knows how it will be when you come down with five small children.' I can still hear her words."

"We would never have left South Africa if not for Uncle Meyer's letter."

"It changed everything," said Sara. "To learn that our whole family in Europe was wiped out, we wanted to be closer to the few that remained."

"It's a pity we had to leave Mr. Garfinkel behind."

ooooo

Sara had not been able to tell anyone about the letter from Abe Garfinkel, though his words floated in her mind day and night. She could now admit that she was in love, but she could no longer hope that they would meet again. The children were adjusting to America and Libka had made the decision to remain at home. How could she uproot them to follow a whim? She was forty-five, after all, and had had her life.

"You told me you wrote Mr. Garfinkel when I was accepted at Cambridge. Did he never answer you, Mom?"

Sara felt that Libka sensed something. She knew her daughter had unusual powers and remembered how on the night the Afrikaner soldier came to kill her, Libka had sprung up in her sleep and dragged her into hiding.

"I will tell you," she now confessed, "he did write me recently."

"And did he tell you about the other woman?"

"There is no other woman."

"I should have known!" Libka fumed. "Mrs. Peker was saying that just to make you feel bad."

On Libka's coaxing, Sara agreed to produce the letter from Abe Garfinkel.

"Can I read it, Mom? Tell me if you'd rather I not."

"You can read."

As Libka read the letter and came to the words, *I will now say what I have felt for a long time: I love you, Sara,* she could no longer control her emotions. Sara too began to cry; and when she reached out to hug her daughter, Libka did not withdraw. She had always felt embarrassed with such displays, but now she allowed it.

Many days passed before they could mention the letter again. Libka felt guilty about rejecting the Cambridge offer. If she would have accepted, perhaps her mother would have moved the family to London and built a life with Mr. Garfinkel.

"I ruined everything for you, Mom," she said one night.

"How did you ruin it?"

"If I went to England, maybe you would have gone too."

"Libka, don't feel responsible. I had a life already. Now my children must build their lives."

"But you're not so old, Mom."

Libka could not accept that her mother's life was over.

"Have you answered Mr. Garfinkel's letter?"

"One day I will answer."

Libka hoped that perhaps the time would come again. If her mother and Mr. Garfinkel were so much in love, maybe it would still be possible for them to be together.

Now that Sara had opened up her heart to her, Libka made an admission.

"I was wrong to be angry with Anya. I should have been happy for her. She had such a miserable life at home and when she finally met a boy she loved, why was I so jealous? I hardly even knew him. And it was stupid of me to turn down Cambridge. Look what I've done to you."

"Don't be so strict with yourself, my child. You are still young and the family is happy that we are all together."

THIRTY-EIGHT

Sara felt that Libka's idea of a weekend in the trailer was unrealistic but the children were so excited that she finally agreed.

"It's like a regular house," Shneyer insisted. "You'll see. It's even nicer than this house."

"I want that house," chimed Dina. "It's even nicer."

Sara arranged for a woman from the Portuguese section to run the laundromat one Saturday. She arose before five and tiptoed downstairs.

Around seven o'clock, when the icebox was filled with sandwiches, drinks, chocolate chip cookies, potato chips and a roast chicken she had made that morning, she crept back up the stairs. She peeked into the room where Libka and Golda slept. Libka's eyes were open, but Sara could not see until she came closer. "You are already up?" She peered into her daughter's face.

"And you've been up for hours. I heard you puttering in the kitchen."

"Everything is ready for the picnic."

"It's not a picnic, Mama. We're going away for the weekend."

Beryl had arranged for the family to use his car and on Friday he took it to the garage to check the air in the tires and the oil level, and he filled the tank with gas.

He knew the area where the trailer stood, for he had sailed past it. As a yachtsman, the idea of sleeping there and awakening to the sunrise excited him. He thought it would be a thrilling excursion for the family. "And, Mom," he said, "you deserve a holiday. It might even remind you of our summers in Muizenberg."

∞∞∞

Cruising along the highway on this Saturday morning, the family felt they were going off on a long journey. Libka was in the drivers' seat, Golda beside her. Sara sat in back with Shneyer and Dina snuggled on either side. The trunk was loaded with the icebox containing their provisions for the weekend, warm clothing and pyjamas for the night, and quilts, pillows and blankets.

This was the first holiday for Sara since coming to America.

Golda began singing "The Rio Grande," and Sara and the children hummed along.

> Oh, say, wuz ye ever down Rio Grande?
> 'Way for Rio!
> It's there that the river flows down golden sands!
> An' we're bound for the Rio Grande...

From a paper bag beside her, Sara produced a handful of plums, offering the juicy fruit to the children.

"It's the nicest house I've ever seen," declared Shneyer. "It's a fun house. I'll show you." Since Shneyer was now seven years old, Sara had agreed to cut his locks, and he felt very grown up.

When Libka veered the car off the highway and took the gravel road toward the sea, the children stood up and peered out. Libka opened her window, allowing the salty breeze to waft into the car. She parked high on the cliff, and they unloaded the trunk and formed a trail as they followed the sandy path. In the distance they could see the trailer, and Shneyer began to run.

The younger children explored every crevice of the trailer as Sara marvelled over the bunk beds and kitchen facilities. She set out the midday meal on the picnic table. She had brought a linoleum cloth, paper plates and plastic cutlery, and Golda helped her lay out the sandwiches and drinks.

After lunch, they changed into their bathing suits and headed for the ocean. Shneyer and Dina splashed near the shore, but Libka dove through a huge breaker, her shiny head popping up in the distance; and Golda swam toward her.

Sara stood at the edge, watching the younger children and occasionally splashing a few drops against her chest.

"Let's get Mom into the water," Libka joked as she and Golda swam back to shore.

When Libka took Sara's hand, she resisted. "No, please leave me."

"Come on," Libka laughed. "Golda, take her other hand."

The sisters tugged Sara into the ocean. As the breakers approached, they lifted her high in the air and she laughed breathlessly, shrieking with joy. "Stop already, children. I will lose my teeth."

By mid-afternoon Shneyer and Dina fell asleep on the bunk beds that Sara had feathered with quilts. Libka and Golda strolled toward a lighthouse, and Sara curled up for a nap on the lower bunk.

The sun was still glorious when they set up the evening meal. After the family had feasted on the roast chicken and potato chips, Libka announced, "Who's for ice cream?"

ooooo

The younger children soon drifted off to sleep. Shneyer was allowed an upper bunk, and Golda lay on the adjoining one, dreaming. Sara covered Dina with the quilt and gazed out of the porthole. She was thinking of a weekend she and the children had spent at Mr. Garfinkel's villa in Camps Bay. Beryl had gone off in the yacht with Simon, Golda and Dina played on the sand, and Shneyer was flying a kite. She was sitting with Abe on the veranda under the palm trees, the birds trilling, the flowers perfuming the air, and he reached for her hand and murmured, "Sara, you have brought me happiness." It was like the dream she had the night before his letter arrived.

ᴏᴏᴏᴏᴏ

As the sunset illuminated the sky, Libka stepped out of the trailer and spread an orange blanket on the sand. The breakers were pounding on the shore, bursting into the sky. It was beside the ocean that she had always found solace. It brought her the strength to bear the loss of her father. And it was the ocean that stirred her with love for the Malay boy.

The full moon seemed to appear for her alone, and she knew where her future lay. She would go to New York and in that larger world she might find the freedom to pursue her dreams. Engraved in her mind was her first glimpse of the great city when she arrived in America and how the passengers had swarmed onto the deck of the vessel as the Statue of Liberty appeared in the New York harbour. They were all filled with hope for a new life, as her family had been.

NOTES

"Die Stem van Suid-Afrika"

Uit die blou van onse he-mel,
Uit die diep-te van ons see,
Oor ons e-wi-ge ge-berg-tes
Waar die kran-se ant-woord gee.

"The Voice of South Africa" (translation)

From the blue of our heaven,
From the depths of our sea,
Over our eternal mountain ranges
Where the cliffs give answer.

The South African national anthem, *"Die Stem van Suid-Afrika"* (The Voice of South Africa), was written by the Afrikaans writer and poet C. J. Langenhoven as a poem in May 1918. In 1921 it was set to music by the Rev. M. L. de Villiers. It was first sung publicly at the official hoisting of the national flag in Cape Town on May 31, 1928.

"There'll Be Bluebirds over the White Cliffs of Dover"

There'll be bluebirds over
The white cliffs of Dover,
Tomorrow, just you wait and see.
There'll be love and laughter
And peace ever after,
Tomorrow, when the world is free...

This is one of the most famous of all the World War II era pop classics. It became a sensational hit in 1942, as it reflected the feelings of all the Allies toward the British people in their brave fight against Hitler.

"God Save the King"

God save our gracious King,
Long live our noble King,
God save the King:
Send him victorious,
Happy and glorious,
Long to reign over us:
God save the King.

The British national anthem, "God Save the King," was often credited to Henry Carey, 1740, although there was controversy with many votes, including the British monarchy's, for anonymous. It was first publicly performed in London in 1745.

"The Rio Grande"

Oh, say, wuz ye ever down Rio Grande?
'Way for Rio!
It's there that the river flows down golden sands!
An' we're bound for the Rio Grande...

"The Rio Grande" was one of the most popular sea shanties. The tune was a capstan or windlass shanty and an outward-bound song. It was commonly sung on ships leaving the West Coast of England and Wales.

ACKNOWLEDGMENTS

In writing this sequel to *In a Pale Blue Light,* I must again pay homage to those who inspired and aided the first book. There was my mother who decades ago, as I was formulating segments for this story, stayed awake half the night reading it. She confirmed that my story is emotionally sound, for the events of which I write were a part of both our lives.

In more recent times I have had special encouragement from two people who remain steadfast in their loyalty: Miriam Beckerman, my literary adviser, a woman with a thirst for knowledge and a passion for books; and Jennifer Day, an editor of incomparable judgment and wisdom.

ABOUT THE AUTHOR

Lily Poritz Miller was born in Cape Town, South Africa, and came to the United States with her family when she was fifteen. After a stint in New York as an actress and playwright, she began her editorial career in book publishing at The Macmillan Company and later McGraw-Hill, then moved to Toronto, where she was senior editor at McClelland and Stewart for eighteen years.

She has written three plays, which were performed in New York and Toronto, and received a Samuel French national award for her play *The Proud One*. Her short stories were published in the anthology *American Scene: New Voices*. She has also written for film. In 2009 her novel *In a Pale Blue Light* was published to critical acclaim. She presently divides her time between Toronto and Mexico.

www.lilyporitzmiller.com